**Her army leave was over in a week, and she was no closer to discovering her stalker's identity than she was three months ago. She was desperate.**

She glared up into those sea-blue eyes of his, her throat constricting. "I thought I made myself perfectly clear. Either you help me find the person stalking me or I go to the military and your clients with what I know about you. And your family."

Facing her oh-so-slowly, Sullivan towered over her, and she fought the urge to take a step back. He leaned in close, mere centimeters from her mouth, as though he intended to kiss her. "Then let me make *myself* perfectly clear. The only way you get my help is if we do this my way, and I plan to get you out of my life as soon as I can."

Jane flinched, but he didn't wait for her to answer, heading for the door.

"Let's go," he said.

# RULES IN BLACKMAIL

―――

## NICHOLE SEVERN

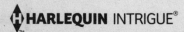

For my husband: couldn't do this without you.

ISBN-13: 978-1-335-63930-1

Rules in Blackmail

Copyright © 2018 by Natascha Jaffa

Recycling programs for this product may not exist in your area.

This edition published by arrangement with Harlequin Books S.A.

For questions and comments about the quality of this book, please contact us at CustomerService@Harlequin.com.

® and TM are trademarks of Harlequin Enterprises Limited or its corporate affiliates. Trademarks indicated with ® are registered in the United States Patent and Trademark Office, the Canadian Intellectual Property Office and in other countries.

Printed in U.S.A.

**Nichole Severn** writes explosive romantic suspense with strong heroines, heroes who dare challenge them and a hell of a lot of guns. She resides with her very supportive and patient husband, as well as her demon spawn, in Utah. When she's not writing, she's constantly injuring herself running, rock climbing, practicing yoga and snowboarding. She loves hearing from readers through her website, www.nicholesevern.com, and on Twitter, @nicholesevern.

## Books by Nichole Severn

### Harlequin Intrigue

*Rules in Blackmail*

Visit the Author Profile page at Harlequin.com.

# CAST OF CHARACTERS

***Sullivan Bishop***—Founder and CEO of Blackhawk Security. Former navy SEAL determined to help those local law enforcement can't or won't. Consumed by his own animosity for Jane Reise, his brother's prosecutor, he doesn't see the threat against Jane's life until it's too late. But when the stalker returns to claim his prize, Sullivan is the only one standing between her and death.

***Jane Reise***—She's the JAG Corps's most promising prosecutor for the army, but the military can't know she's being stalked or she'll lose her security clearance. She's forced to blackmail her last resort for help: Sullivan Bishop, the brother of a man she prosecuted in Afghanistan. Only she knows who Sullivan really is and what he's been hiding, and she'll do whatever it takes to survive.

***Elliot Dunham***—Blackhawk Security's con man turned private investigator. Swiped off the Iraqi streets right after Sullivan's discharge from the SEALs. He has a knack for finding and recovering classified documents, digging into a person's life and discovering those secrets his target doesn't want the world to know about.

***Anthony Harris***—Weapons expert for Blackhawk Security. Specializes in reconnaissance, intelligence gathering, raids, recovery and security. As a former army ranger, he's one of the most trusted men on Sullivan's team.

***Marrok Warren***—Sullivan's brother, who was prosecuted by Jane for sexual assault of three separate women while on tour in Afghanistan. Staff Sergeant Warren committed suicide after the court-martial, which Sullivan blames on Jane.

***Christopher Menas***—Jane's college ex-boyfriend, the center of their investigation into who is stalking Jane. He escaped sentencing for sexual assault of her roommates after she turned him in to the police ten years ago. Now Christopher is back, looking for his revenge.

# *Chapter One*

"You have exactly five seconds to talk, or I start shooting." Sullivan Bishop slipped his finger alongside the gun's trigger.

"I'm not armed." The woman in his sights raised her hands to shoulder level, but didn't make another move. She might've been pretty, but in his experience, pretty faces were the best at hiding lies. And the lean dark-haired woman standing in the middle of his office had one of the prettiest faces he'd ever seen. Knowing her, she'd come armed. "I want to talk. Figured this would be the best place to do it."

He balanced his weight between both feet. His heart pumped hard as he tightened his grip around the Glock. How long had it been since Jane Reise—the legendary JAG Corps prosecutor herself—had crossed his mind? Nine months? Ten? Didn't matter. Nobody uninvited strolled into Blackhawk Security and stepped back through those doors without answering for something.

Jane had a lot to answer for.

"And you thought breaking into my private security company after hours was your best plan? How the hell did you get in here?" Sullivan closed in on her one inch at a time while he listened for movement on the rest of the floor. How had she gotten past his security system? Blackhawk Security provided top-of-the-line security measures, including cameras, body-heat sensors, motion detectors and more. Whatever the client needed, they delivered. Sometimes those services included personal protection, investigating, logistical support to the US government and personal recovery. They did it all. But right now, his gut instincts were telling him Jane wasn't standing in his office for some added security around her town house.

"Would you believe me if I said I came to hire you?" She swiped her tongue over her full bottom lip. Dropping her hands to her side, she scanned the rest of the office and widened her stance. Moonlight, coming through the wall of windows looking over downtown Anchorage, splayed across one half of her face. It washed out the brilliant color of her hazel eyes he'd studied from her file all those months ago. She was far more beautiful in person—no argument there—but the cord of tension stiffening her neck darkened her features.

"You're kidding, right?" This was a joke. Had to be. Sullivan stopped no more than five feet from her, a quick burst of laughter rumbling through his chest. The gun grew heavy in his hand. He lowered it to his side but wouldn't holster the Glock until he was certain she'd come unarmed. "I'm the last person on this planet who'd help you."

Jane scanned the office a second time, looking everywhere but at him. Even in the dark, Sullivan swore the color drained from her face.

"I never meant…" She cleared her throat, determination wiping away the momentary fall of her features. "You have every reason to laugh in my face and shove me out the door, but I don't have anywhere else to go. The police don't have any leads, and I can't get the army involved. Not yet."

"Involved in what?" Flipping on the overhead lights, Sullivan saw what she'd tried to hide by sticking to the shadows of his office. She squinted against the onslaught of brightness. Dark circles had taken up residence under her eyes, a sort of hollowness thinning her cheeks. Her normally athletic and lean frame seemed smaller than he remembered from her photos, as though she'd lost not only weight but any muscle she'd gained from her current stint in the army. The white T-shirt and black cargo jacket washed color from her skin but didn't detract from her overall beauty. Still, something was wrong. This wasn't the same woman who'd stood in front of a judge a year ago and ripped apart his family.

"I'm being watched." The corner of her mouth twitched as though she were biting the inside of her cheek. Her shoulders rose on a deep inhale. "Stalked."

The fear in her voice twisted his insides—would twist any man's insides—but Sullivan didn't respond. It was a counterintelligence tactic. Keep your mouth shut, and the target was more likely to fill the silence. If she was lying, he'd know by the way her eyes darted to the left or how she held her arms around her middle.

"They've been in my house and my car. I don't know where else." Jane brushed a piece of short dark hair behind her ear and the strong, confident woman he'd studied from the surveillance photos and video taken during the trial disappeared. "If the army knew about this, they'd limit my security clearance, and I could lose my job. I called in an anonymous tip to the police, but—"

"The case isn't high on their list." He understood the way the Anchorage Police Department worked. Until there was an actual threat on Jane's life, they had more important cases to work. That'd been one of the reasons Sullivan had founded Blackhawk Security in the first place. Aside from providing investigative services for government officials and witnesses to crimes, his team protected victims law enforcement couldn't. Or wouldn't. But taking on Jane's case...

She wasn't lying, at least not from what he could tell, but helping her wasn't exactly high on his priority list either. "Do you have proof?"

With a quick nod of her perfectly angled chin, she drew her cell phone from her jacket pocket, swiping her finger across the screen. A few more clicks and she offered him the phone. "I found this picture of me sleeping in my bed yesterday morning. It's dated two nights ago, around midnight."

He took the phone from her and his index finger brushed against the side of her hand. The lack of warmth in her skin caught his attention, and he pulled back. Studying the photo taken with her own phone, Sullivan fought the urge to tighten his grip on the device. The idea of a man—any man—taking photos of a woman without her permission built pressure behind his sternum. A woman shouldn't be afraid, shouldn't have to look over her shoulder. Not ever. "Any ideas of who could've broken in?"

"No." Her defeated answer wisped out from between her lips, drawing his attention up. Eyes wide, she shook her head slightly. "I live alone."

Then, barring a random break-in, she most definitely had a stalker. Handing the phone back to her, Sullivan ensured his fingers didn't touch hers again. His insides had already caught fire from an intruder breaking into his highly secure office. He didn't need anything else clouding his head. "Does anyone else have a key to your apartment? Maybe an old boyfriend who hasn't gotten the idea you two are over?"

With another shake of her head, her hair swung slightly below her earlobes. "No. I don't..." Jane cocked her head to the side as she shrugged. "I don't have any old boyfriends. Not since I went into the army."

Which was five years ago, according to her military record. Sullivan's fingers twitched at his side. "And what about your case files? Anyone not—" he ground his back teeth "—*happy* with the way you handled their case?"

Aside from him, that was.

Her lips thinned as she rolled them between her teeth. "Not that I know of, but I have all the files for the cases I was assigned back at my house if you want to go through them."

Not going to happen. He shoved the Glock into his shoulder holster, the adrenaline rush draining from his veins. Despite getting past his security system, Jane wasn't a threat. Yet. "That won't be necessary."

"Okay, what then?" She rolled her shoulders back but didn't move otherwise. Did she realize how much he blamed her for what happened and didn't want to take the chance of getting close? He liked to think so. She'd prosecuted dozens of devoted soldiers—men and women who'd sworn to protect this country, men like him—and she wanted his help? The woman was insane.

Captain Jane Reise was responsible for his brother's suicide. She didn't deserve an ounce of pity from him.

Spinning toward his desk, he grabbed a pad of paper and a pen. "This is the name of another security consultant to handle your case. I suggest you give him a call and get out of my office."

"I came here because I need *your* help."

Hints of that legendary prosecutor he'd studied bled into her voice. Her sweet scent of vanilla climbed down into his lungs and he forced himself to hold his breath. "Isn't that what Blackhawk Security does? Help people?"

"Yes." Sullivan ripped the note from the pad and handed it to her. He spun away from those far too intelligent eyes and headed for the door. Turning the knob, he swung it open and motioned her out. "But not you."

Crossing her arms, Jane leveled her chin to the floor and sat back against the desk. Every cell in his body stood at attention as fire bled into her gaze. "I'm not leaving until you agree to help me."

"Move. Or I'll throw you over my shoulder and dump you in the hallway." He liked the visual. Far too much. He shouldn't, but damn it he did. All that soft skin, her lean frame wrapped around his, her hair tickling him across his back. Sullivan shut down that line of thought. Didn't matter how fiery or intelligent she was or how much she begged for his help. Wasn't going to happen. Ever. He crossed his arms over his chest, parroting her movement. Even from this distance, he noted her throat constricting on a slow swallow. "Get out."

"I can pay you." She pushed off from the desk. "Anything you want."

"This isn't about money." Sullivan dropped his hold on the door. Marching across the room, he shortened the space between them until she had to look up at him.

Her chin notched higher as she held her ground.

The woman had stood up to all kinds of criminals and soldiers over the years. She wasn't intimidated. Damn if that wasn't the sexiest thing he'd ever seen. But he knew better than to trust her.

Chest almost pressed against her, he quirked one corner of his mouth. There were other ways to get her out of his office. He pushed his palms on either side of her on the desk, leaning down. "Unless you're talking about something other than money…"

Her lips parted, a sharp exhale of air beating against him. Jane studied his face from top to bottom but didn't move to escape the box he'd created around her. She locked that striking gaze on his, eyes determined and wide. "Dollars and cents, Lieutenant Bishop. Nothing more."

"Then you'll want to leave before I put in a call to your commanding officer and have you disbarred for harassing the family of one of your victims." He shoved himself away from the desk, away from that intoxicating scent of hers, and headed toward the door.

"I can make you help me," she said.

Another rush of heat overwhelmed his control, and he stopped dead in his tracks. What part of his answer didn't she understand? He spun back toward her. If it was a fight she was looking for, fine. He had no problem taking down the woman who'd destroyed his family. He might even enjoy it. "I'd like to see you try."

"All right." Jane straightened her spine as though she was preparing for battle. That same fire he'd caught a glimpse of during his brother's court-martial encroached on the darkness embedded in her features. "I know who you really are. And I know what you've been hiding."

"You don't know anything about me." Sullivan Bishop seemed so much...*bigger* than he had a moment ago. Caged by his body against the desk, she felt his heat tunnel through her clothing. Hatred had burned in those sea-colored eyes as he'd pressed his chest against hers.

Jane swallowed as he stretched his shoulders wider. What had she been thinking to try to blackmail a man like him? Blackhawk Security's CEO wasn't an administrator over a team of highly trained ex-military operatives. He *was* ex-military. He'd been a SEAL, capable of the worst kind of violence. And she'd just threatened everything he'd ever worked for.

He closed in on her a second time. His clean, fresh scent whispered across the underside of her jaw as he spoke.

The hairs on the back of her neck stood on end. Every word out of his mouth promised she was going to wish she hadn't gone down this path, but Jane didn't have any other choice. Gliding her tongue across her bottom lip—a movement his eyes locked onto—she stood her ground. There was no turning back. He was the best, and she needed his help. One way or another.

"I know Sullivan Bishop isn't your real name." Every muscle in his body tightened in warning, and Jane forced herself to breathe evenly. She pressed her lower back into the desk. "And the people holding your company's military contracts might be interested to know why you changed it. A few of your classified clients, too, I imagine."

"You're blackmailing me?" A low growl reverberated up his throat and hiked her blood pressure higher. The shadows angling across the dark, thick stubble darkening his jaw shifted, but those sea-blue eyes never left hers. The veins in his arms popped as he leaned into her, the butt of the Glock in his shoulder holster pressing into her arm. "Are you sure you want to go down this road, Captain Reise? It won't end well."

"I'm willing to do whatever it takes to survive." A shiver chased up her spine, but Jane held her ground. She couldn't live like this anymore. The late-night phone calls, the feeling of being watched, the sick photo in her cell phone of her sleeping. And there was more. Going back several weeks. "Have you ever been hunted like an animal, Lieutenant Bishop?"

The suffocating bubble of tension he'd built around her disappeared. The edge to his features softened. She breathed a little easier. Putting some distance between them, Sullivan relaxed his hands to his sides, but the strong muscles flexing the length of his arms promised he was fully capable of violence. "Yes."

"Then you know what it's like to constantly be looking over your shoulder, to feel so helpless you don't seem to have any control of your own life." She crossed her arms over her chest, fully aware of the loss of body heat he'd forced through her with his proximity. Her hands shook as the terror she'd tried keeping to herself crept through her. "To feel like every second you're alive could actually be your last."

The lines running from the edge of his nose to those perfectly crafted lips deepened. She couldn't read his expression, but the tension in his neck and shoulders released.

"How did you get through it?" she asked.

Sullivan's chest expanded on a deep inhale. At least he wasn't crowding her anymore. She could actually breathe again, but the cold fist tightened in the pit of her stomach. "I have people I trust to back me up no matter what the situation calls for."

She nodded. That was what she was counting on. Why she was here in the first place. Sullivan had the reputation for committing himself to every job he took on, and while it was a risk to rely on the man she was blackmailing, she hoped his reputation proved true. "Well, I don't have a team. I have you. And if it's going to take blackmail to get you to help me, then so be it."

Silence pressed in on her as Sullivan studied her from head to toe. A scorching trail of awareness skittered across her skin. What did he see? A woman who couldn't protect herself? Or the woman responsible for his brother's death?

"I'll give you twenty-four hours of my time," he said. "After that, you can go back to your cold, empty existence and leave me the hell alone."

He was just like the rest of them: her peers, the men and women she prosecuted to protect citizens of the United States, even her commanding officer. She'd earned her reputation as the Full Metal B, she supposed. Her job required an almost ruthless approach to the cases she'd been assigned, but this was the first time her rib cage tightened at someone's assessment of her. Which didn't make sense. She didn't care what Sullivan Bishop thought of her. She didn't care what any of them thought of her. Her insides twisted. She didn't care. Jane shoved off from the massive desk he'd trapped her against moments before. Uncrossing her arms, she stepped toward him. "So you'll help mc?"

"I don't have a choice, do I? Isn't that how blackmail is supposed to work?" Sullivan rounded his desk. The thick muscles across his back flexed through his shirt. She forced her attention to the sway of his gun rather than the way he moved, to prove she could take her eyes off him. Lean waist, strong legs, hints of his trident tattoo peeking out from under his T-shirt. Such a dangerous man shouldn't be that attractive. "We'll take my car."

Jane straightened. Okay. They were doing this. "Where are we going?"

"To your town house. I'll brief my team on the way." He unholstered the Glock from his side and dropped the magazine into his hand. After a glance at the rounds, he replaced it with efficient, sure movements and chambered a round. He raised that piercing gaze to hers. "I have a man on my team who used to work forensics for the NYPD. If your stalker has been in your house like you claim, he'll find the evidence and we can all move on with our lives."

She ran her cold palms over the front of her jeans and took another step toward him. He was actually going to help her find the man trying to destroy her life? A knot of hope pulsed from deep in her chest. "And if he does find evidence? What then?"

Sullivan came around the desk, his wide shoulders blocking out the magnificent view of the Chugach mountain range behind him. Nearly pressing against her, he stared down at her. At six foot four, it wasn't hard, but the intimidation had drained from his body. He stalked toward the office door. "Then you'll have the proof you need to take to the police."

"What?" Jane wrapped her hand halfway around his massive biceps and spun him around to look at her. He'd let her. She didn't have the strength to move a mountain like him. She was at the end of her rope, and she hadn't come here to admit defeat. Her leave ended in a week, and she'd come no closer to discovering her stalker's identity than she was three months ago. Desperation held her tight.

She glared up into those sea-blue eyes of his, her throat constricting. "I thought I made myself perfectly clear. Either *you* help me find the person stalking me or I go to the government and your clients with what I know about you. And your family."

Facing her, oh-so-slowly, Sullivan towered over her, and she fought the urge to take a step back. He leaned in close, mere centimeters from her mouth, as though he intended to kiss her. "Then let me make myself perfectly clear. The only way you get my help is if we do this my way, and I plan to get you out of my life as soon as I can."

Jane flinched, but he didn't wait for her to answer, heading for the door.

"Let's go," he said.

This was a mistake. She should've known how deep Sullivan's hatred for her flowed, but she'd run out of options. Jane followed on his heels toward the elevator, allowing a good amount of distance between them as they crowded into the small space on the way down to the parking garage. Neither said a word. His clean scent wrapped around her, and she gripped the handrail to clear her head. In less than a minute, he led her out of the elevator and across the empty parking garage toward a black SUV.

Tingling spread across her back—an all-too-familiar feeling—and Jane turned back toward the elevator, heart in her throat. Darkness surrounded them. Everyone in the building had already gone home for the day. She'd made sure. Everyone except Sullivan and a few security guards, but someone else was here. *He* was here, watching her. She felt it.

"Jane." Sullivan's deep timbre flooded her nerves with relief, but she couldn't shake the feeling they were being watched. "Jane," he said again.

She stared at him. It was her imagination. Had to be. There was no way anyone could've followed her here. She'd been too careful, but still, the sensation between her shoulder blades prickled her instincts. "I'm coming."

Sullivan ripped open the driver's-side door of

the large black SUV, his eyes sweeping across the parking garage as she moved to the other side. Once she was safely inside the car, the sensation disappeared and Jane breathed a bit easier. Nobody had been watching her. The constant paranoia had just become a habit.

Sullivan slammed the door behind him and started the engine. Black leather and dark interiors gave her a false sense of security, but having him in the driver's seat eased some of the tension on either side of her spine. At the exit, he lowered the window and scanned his key card. Nobody went in or out of the garage without a card. He swung the SUV north through an area of warehouses and railroads, as though he knew exactly where they were headed.

The SUV plowed through the wet streets of downtown Anchorage, spitting up water and snow along the way. The heater chased away the ice that'd built inside her over the past few weeks. She was reminded of Sullivan's heat back in his office. The same heat rolled off him in waves now. She watched him from her peripheral vision. He wore only a T-shirt and jeans in these temperatures, a human furnace. It'd been too long since she'd felt anything but fear.

"I know what you've heard about me, what they called me in Afghanistan. I'm not as cold as you think." Sitting straighter in her seat, Jane stared down into her lap to counteract the need to explain herself to Blackhawk Security's CEO. "I didn't want to dig into your history. I needed—"

"We're not doing this right now," he said, one hand on the wheel. He still wouldn't look at her. Typical alpha male, determined not to talk. Sullivan pressed his foot on the accelerator as they rolled onto the bridge across Knik Arm, the shallow water almost motionless with a few inches of ice across the top.

"All right." She wiped her clammy hands down her thighs. "Tough crowd."

A light falling of snow peppered the windshield. Nothing like the storms Anchorage usually saw this time of year, but just as beautiful as she remembered growing up in Seattle.

The high screech of peeling tires broke their self-imposed silence, and Jane swept her gaze out the window. Blinded by fast-approaching headlights, she shoved away from the door as a truck slammed into her side of the SUV.

# Chapter Two

The loud groan of a truck's engine brought Sullivan around.

"Reise?" Pain. In his skull. Everywhere. He blinked to clear his vision and ran his hand over his left cheek. Something warm and sticky coated his hand. Blood. He fought to scan his body for other injuries. Hell. They'd flipped.

Cracks in the windshield spidered out in a dendritic pattern, blocking his view of the other driver. Had they survived? Been injured? He depressed the seat belt button and collapsed onto the SUV's roof. Broken glass from the window cut into him. He pounded his fist into the roof and locked his jaw. "Damn it!"

He swiped blood from his eyes. Where was Jane? Twisting inside the crushed interior, he spotted her. Sullivan crawled through debris and around the middle console, ignoring the pain screaming for his attention. The seat belt held her in the passenger seat, upside down. Couldn't search her for injuries here. They needed to get clear of the wreck. "Captain Reise, can you hear me?"

She didn't respond, unconscious.

Bracing himself, Sullivan released her belt and caught her just before she hit the SUV's roof. He pressed his palm against the glistening gash across the right side of her head to stop the bleeding, then checked her slender neck for a pulse. Thready, but there.

Burning rubber and exhaust worked down into his lungs. Crouching low to see through the passenger-side window, he kept pressure on her wound. But couldn't hold it for long. The yellow tow truck's tires screeched again as it made another lunge straight for them.

"You've got to be kidding me." His fight-or-flight instinct kicked into high gear. Heaving Jane across the cab, he pulled her through his shattered driver's-side window with everything he had. They cleared the SUV, but his momentum catapulted them down the steep embankment surrounding the shallow water of Knik Arm.

The world spun as snow and mud worked under his clothes and clung tight to his skin and hair. His arms closed around Jane, the movement as natural as breathing as they rolled. They slammed into a nearby tree, mere feet from the ice-cold water of the river. Positioned on top of her, he scanned her once more, panting. His vision split into two and he shook his head.

He leveraged his weight into the palms of his hands to give her more breathing room, his heart pumping hard. "Captain Reise, wake up. We need to—"

The second crash forced Sullivan's gaze up the snow-covered hill. The SUV's headlights flickered a split second before the entire vehicle started to slide down the slope, heading right for them. There was no time to think. He dug his fingertips into Jane's arm and spun them through the snow and weeds to the right as fast as he could. The SUV sped past, breaking through the six inches of solid ice at the edge of the river.

Hell. This wasn't some freak accident. Someone wasn't just stalking Jane. They'd now decided they wanted her dead. He studied the cut across her head, then her sharp features. She'd been telling the truth. Sullivan exhaled hard. Puffs of breath crystallized in front of his mouth. "Come on, Jane. We have to get out of here."

Jane? When had he started calling her by her first name?

Screeching tires above echoed in his ears as the tow truck hauled fast away from the scene. *Damn it.* He hadn't seen the driver at all. He could still catch up. He could—

Jane moaned as she stirred in his arms. Her lips parted. Such soft, pink lips. Pulse now beating steady at the base of her throat, she fought to focus on him. She lifted one hand toward her face, but he wrapped his fingers around her small wrist. "What…happened? My head—" She locked her fuzzy gaze on him. "Did you just call me Jane instead of Captain Reise?"

He swallowed. She'd heard that? "You hit your head pretty hard against the window when the truck slammed into us. Must've heard me wrong."

Sullivan shoved a strand of her hair out of her face to see her wound better. Her features softened as she closed her eyes. She was okay as far as he could tell, but the spike of adrenaline had yet to drain from his system. Whoever had been driving that truck had made a very dangerous enemy. Not only had he gone after an unarmed woman, he'd tried killing the CEO of the government's most resourced private security contractor. No way Sullivan was going to turn Jane's case over to Anchorage PD now. That bastard was his.

"What happened?" Those brilliant hazel eyes swept over the embankment, and he noted exactly when Jane caught sight of the totaled SUV. Every muscle down her spine tightened as she dug her heels into the snow to sit up. "Somebody tried to kill us."

No point in denying the facts. Her stalker had gone from hunting Jane in her own home to outright attempted murder. "Looks that way. Can you stand?"

She nodded, rolling her upper body off the ground, but grabbed for his arm. Stinging heat splintered through his muscles where she touched him, his bare skin exposed to the dropping temperatures.

"It'll be light soon." Sullivan tugged his arm from her grasp as he scanned their surroundings. They hadn't made it too far from downtown, but he couldn't take the chance of taking her back to the office. Her stalker had known exactly where to find them, as if he'd been waiting. Might've been on her tail when Jane had broken into Blackhawk Security. Whoever it was, the guy was willing to kill bystanders to get to her, which meant they couldn't go to her town house either. "We don't want to be caught out here overnight."

"There's nowhere we can hide." Her teeth

chattered together as she wrapped her arms around her midsection. She stared at the half-sunken SUV, shaking her head. "I was careful. I made sure no one was following me when I went to your office. I made sure..." Her words left her mouth quick and breathless as she finally looked at him. "He wants me dead."

His insides flipped, and Sullivan reached for her without thinking. He pulled her into his chest. At about five foot three, Jane barely came to his sternum, but she fitted. Fragile, vulnerable, but strong. His back molars clamped together, jaw straining. She'd ripped apart his family. She was even blackmailing him into protecting her, but the fear darkening those eyes had urged him to lock her body against his automatically. Her job might've made her a few enemies, but not even the army's most revered prosecutor deserved to be hunted like an animal. No one did.

Tremors racked through her—most likely shock—but he dropped his hold. Wisps of her sweet scent replaced the smell of exhaust and burned rubber seared into his memory, and he inhaled deeply to clear his system. They had to get moving. "Whoever this guy is, we'll find him."

The shivers simmered. Sliding her hands between their bodies, she placed them above his heart and tilted her head back to look up at him. "Thank you."

Heat worked through his chest, a combination of dropping temperatures and the rage he held for her fighting for his attention. Her nearly dying at the hands of a crazed psychopath wouldn't change the past between them. Nothing could.

"For getting me out of the SUV, I mean." Cuts, scrapes and dried blood marred her otherwise flawless skin, a small bruise forming on the right side of her face. A strand of short black hair slid along the curve of her cheek, but he wouldn't brush it away. "You could've left me there to take care of your blackmail problem, but you didn't. I appreciate that."

He kept his expression tight. Right. Jane Reise had the power to bring down his entire company with one phone call and had made it perfectly clear she was willing to use it. How could he have forgotten?

"Yeah, well, whoever you pissed off tried to kill me, and you're the only lead I have to hunt him down." Sullivan put some much-needed space between them. She'd most certainly lived up to her reputation in the last hour they'd been forced together. He curled his fingers into his palms to douse the urge to comfort her. The woman who'd destroyed his family—the woman *blackmailing* him for his help—didn't deserve comfort. And she wouldn't get it from him. He had control. Time to use it.

"Right." Jane's throat constricted on a hard swallow. She shoved her hands into her jacket pockets and surveyed their surroundings. "I'd say call a tow truck, but I think your SUV is beyond saving."

Cracking ice pulled his attention toward the river. The SUV was sinking. In less than five minutes, the entire vehicle would be submerged in the icy Gulf of Alaska. Treading through six inches of muddy snow toward the vehicle, Sullivan registered her confident footsteps behind him. He hauled the tailgate above his head and tossed the false bottom of the trunk to his right. "Now we're on foot. Take this." He thrust the lighter duffel bag from the trunk at Jane. He grabbed a thick coat and the heavier bag for himself. Boy Scouts, SEALs and Alaskans all had one motto in common: Never Get Caught in the Wilderness Unprepared.

She unzipped the bag he'd handed her. "Food and guns. You're officially the man of my dreams."

She'd meant it as a joke, but, hell, the compliment forced him to pause.

"Wait until you see what's in this bag. Between us, we'll be able to survive out here for at least three days." He didn't bother closing the tailgate. Some civilian would drive past and put a call in to the cops, or the SUV would sink. Either way, he and Jane weren't sticking around to find out. He couldn't take the risk of her stalker coming back to the scene to make sure the job was done. "We're heading northeast." He pointed toward the thick outcropping of trees as he pulled on his thick coat. "It's a three-mile hike. We need to leave now in case your stalker realizes he didn't finish the job."

"Where are we going?" She brought up the hood on her cargo jacket. Smart move. The Alaskan wilderness wasn't any place to screw around. They had to stay warm and dry or risk hypothermia.

Sullivan covered his head to conserve body heat. A gust of freezing wind whipped one side of his body as he headed into the forest. "Somewhere no one will find us."

HE'D CALLED HER Jane back on the embankment. Not Captain Reise. She'd heard him clear as day. Because even in the midst of suffocating unconsciousness, Jane had locked on to his voice. The man she was blackmailing had brought her out of the darkness. Why? He had no allegiance to her.

Sullivan cleared a path through the thickest parts of the forest with one of the extra blades from his duffel bag a few feet up ahead of her. Shadows cast across his features from the beam from his flashlight. Snow had worked down into her boots, turning to slush. Her jeans were soaked through. How long had they been out here? An hour? Two? Three miles didn't seem like much until deep snow and freezing temperatures added to the misery. Not to mention it was dark and difficult to see. Her toes had gone numb long ago, fingers following close behind, but Jane kept her mouth shut. They had to be close, right? She swiped away a few drops of water from her cheek, wincing as pain radiated up toward her temple. The sooner they made it to their destination—wherever that was— the better.

Distraction. She had to keep her mind off her frozen limbs. "Bet you've never had to walk through the Alaskan wilderness with a client to escape a crazed psychopath before."

"You're right." He laughed, a deep guttural rumble she felt down into her bones. It was real, warming. Swinging his arm out, he held back a large branch so she could pass. He stared down at her while she maneuvered around him, those sea-blue eyes brightening in the muted beam from his flashlight. "I usually reserve these kinds of trips for people I've been assigned to hunt down."

"Is that a nice way of putting that you've killed people for a living?" She instantly regretted the words, and her heart rate rocketed. "I mean, I read your military record during the trial. I know you used to be a SEAL, one of the best. You don't have to lie to me or sugarcoat anything."

"Once a SEAL, always a SEAL. You never really retire. It stays in your blood, makes you who you are. Forever." Defensiveness tinted his words as Jane followed in his sunken footsteps. But, faster than she thought possible, he latched onto her arm and spun her into his chest. The hard set to his eyes said Sullivan Bishop could be a very dangerous enemy, but she'd known that before throwing his secrets in his face. Right now, in this moment, her instincts said he wouldn't hurt her. She'd learned to trust those instincts to get her through the past few years. "And, as a prosecutor, you of all people should understand that the best defense against evil men is good men who deal in violence."

Jane took a deep breath. One, two. She

couldn't get enough air. Staring up at him, she noted the gash across his cheek he must've suffered during the wreck. He'd protected her back there because she was a lead. Nothing more. He'd said as much, but why did being this close to him change her breathing patterns? "And what about now?"

"What do you mean?" Sullivan narrowed his eyes, his features turning to stone.

"Do you still 'hunt down' people for a living?" she asked.

Seconds ticked by, then a minute. Something in her heart froze. Sullivan was a killer. It'd been part of the job description, part of his past, but Jane couldn't keep track of how long he held her there as snow fell from branches around them. His mesmerizing gaze held hers, but Jane had a feeling he wasn't really seeing her at all. His fingers dug into her, keeping his hold light enough not to bruise. He wasn't trying to hurt her. Maybe...he didn't want to let her go.

"Isn't that why you blackmailed me into helping you?" The demons were evident in his eyes, but Sullivan released his grip on her arm and put a few inches of freezing Alaska air between them as he turned his back on her and pushed forward.

"No. I blackmailed you to find the man doing

this to me so we can turn him over to the police." Her skin tingled through her thin coat where he'd latched onto her arm. Phantom sensations. There was no way he could affect her like that. Not in these temperatures. She studied him from behind, the way his back stretched each time he took a step, the way he carried himself as though nothing could get through him if a threat arose. "I'm sorry. I didn't mean to…"

What? Pry into his life? Doubt his reasons for doing what needed to be done overseas and here in the United States?

Pushing on up ahead, he worked to clear branches. After a few seconds, Sullivan halted in his tracks, turning back toward her. Stubble speckled with ice and snow, he swayed on his feet. Good to know she wasn't the only one suffering from exhaustion. He scanned over her from head to toe. "Don't worry about it."

"I appreciate everything you've done for your country and what you're doing now. I'm sure every American does. It's admirable." She fought for a full lungful of air. Despite the dropping temperatures, her skin heated when he looked at her like that. Like she was a threat. She stepped over the remnants of a few branches he'd demolished along the way, nearly losing her footing. In that moment, something between them shifted. An understanding of sorts. No messy blackmail. No psychotic lunatic trying to run them down with his tow truck. Not even security consultant and client. Just two people trying to survive in the middle of the Alaskan wilderness. Together. "You don't have to do all this work yourself, you know. I can help."

"You're more than welcome to…" His mouth went slack as though he couldn't get enough oxygen. Probably couldn't. Freezing temperatures didn't discriminate against SEALs or lawyers. Mother Nature treated everyone equally.

"Are you okay?" she asked. "Sullivan?"

They'd crossed at least two and a half miles of heavy snow and growth, maybe more. She was tired and couldn't feel her toes, but her instincts urged her to get to him. Now.

Sullivan doubled over, dropping his gear before he collapsed onto his side.

"Sullivan!" Jane discarded the duffel bag and lunged toward him. Her feet felt like frozen blocks of ice, but she fought the piling snow with everything she had. Hands outstretched, she checked his pulse. Weak. "No, no, no, no. Come on. Get up."

Gripping his jawline, she brought one ear to

his mouth. Still breathing. Would anyone hear her out here? "Help!"

Sullivan Bishop was a SEAL, for crying out loud. This shouldn't be happening. He'd trained for situations exactly like this. Her heart beat out of control. She dived for the duffel bag he'd been carrying. Food, more guns. There had to be a—

"Yes!" She ripped the first-aid kit from the bag, fought to break the seal on the space blanket, then covered him completely. The hand and foot warmers were easier to open with her stiff fingers, but they wouldn't be enough. One look at Sullivan's normally full, sensual pink lips said she was running out of time. She had to get his body temperature up before hypothermia set in, but the blanket and a few warmers wouldn't cut it.

"You are not allowed to die on me. You hear me? I can't do this without you. You're going to listen to my voice and wake up so I don't have to carry you." Scanning the thick trees ahead of their location, Jane narrowed in on a clearing. And across that? A small cabin set into the other side of the trees. Had to be Sullivan's safe house. Had to be. If not, they'd at least have some protection from the elements while the owners called for help. "You're going to make me drag you there, aren't you?"

She didn't have time to wait for an answer. Leaving the duffel bags, Jane fisted her numb grip into his jacket and pulled. The snow eased the friction underneath him as she hefted Sullivan toward the clearing, but her strength gave out after only a few hundred feet. She collapsed back into the snow, fingers aching, heart racing. Hours upon hours of training kept her in shape in the army, but this? This was different. And the security contractor at her feet wasn't exactly a lightweight. "Come on, Sullivan. Think lighter thoughts."

The trees passed by in a blur. She couldn't focus on anything but shoving one foot back behind the other. Minutes passed, hours it seemed, and they hit the clearing. Only a few hundred more feet and faster than she thought possible, the heels of her boots knocked against the steps leading into the cabin. She tried the door. Locked. Pounding her fists against the door, she listened carefully for movement, but no one answered. In a rush, she searched for a fake rock, anything that would get her inside. She hunted around the bushes and flitted over something that was most certainly not natural: a key taped to one of the thick branches. Shoving the steel into the dead bolt and turning, she sighed in victory.

Heat enveloped her in seconds, thawing her fingers in a rush until they burned. No time. She spun back to Sullivan and slid her grip under his arms. An exhausted groan broke free from her lips as she hauled him inside. Fire. She had to start a fire to get him warm.

"Almost there. Hang on." Throwing off her coat, Jane ran toward the fireplace and got a small fire going. She'd add more to it in a few minutes, but right now, Sullivan's wet clothes and his own sweat were doing his body more harm than good. She stripped off her coat, socks and jeans, staring down at the peaceful expression settled across his strong, handsome features. Then it was his turn.

"Sorry, Sullivan. You might hate me even more after you wake up." Crouching at his feet, she untied his boot laces and unbuttoned his pants. Jane hefted her own shirt over her head, adding it to the pile of clothes at her feet. Tugging him up into a sitting position, she stripped him down to nothing. "But it's going to save your life."

# Chapter Three

Dying hurt like hell.

Heat blistered along his forearms, neck and face. His entire body ached in places he hadn't thought about since his SEAL days. He hadn't been on active duty for over a year now, but Sullivan still trained as though he were. Had to be ready for anything his clients might throw his way. Even the beginning stages of hypothermia. Damn it, he should've known better. Groaning, he cracked open his eyes, stomach still rolling. A fire popped a few feet from him.

At least he knew where he was. The cabin was sparse: one bedroom, one bath, a living room and small kitchen. He mostly came out here when he wanted to be alone, needed to get away from people, the city or both. No neighbors, no one to encroach on his business. And he'd never brought anyone here before. He'd kept this place under his mother's maiden name in case he'd needed a safe house. It couldn't be traced back to him if Jane's stalker—or anyone else—had the inclination to investigate. But how in the hell did he get here?

Sullivan raised his head. He wasn't alone.

Endless amounts of warm, smooth skin stretched out beside him under the heaviest blanket he kept on hand in the cabin. A head of black hair rested against his right arm. Jane? He had to be dreaming. Skimming his fingers across her shoulder blade, he sank into how very real she felt. Nope. Not a dream. But why would she… The lapse in his memory filled almost instantly. The last thing he remembered was the look on her face as he…collapsed. Terrified. Hell. Had she dragged him all the way out here on her own?

Her shoulders rising and falling against him in a slow, even rhythm said she was fast asleep. He couldn't have been out for long. An hour— two, tops—from the amount of moonlight coming through the front room window. He'd messed up out there, but her sultry vanilla scent spared him a few ounces of guilt. It dived into his lungs, and he took a deep breath to keep it in his system as long as possible. His heart rate dropped to a slow, even thump behind his ears.

He closed his eyes, all too easily seeing himself burying his nose in her hair for another round.

Nope. Not the time and definitely not this woman.

Sullivan shifted his hips away from her backside. If Jane woke up now, there'd be no hiding what was going on downstairs in that moment. His brain might have control, but with the expanse of soft skin along his front, his body had other ideas. He scanned the living room and spotted his clothes hanging from fishing line around the open rafters by the fireplace. He'd gotten out of some real complicated situations in the navy. There had to be a way to unwind himself from this warm, coldhearted woman without waking her.

He leveraged his weight into his toes and stretched out his arm. A soft, guttural moan worked up Jane's throat. Something primal washed through him. He froze. There was a stalker on the loose and he'd nearly died out in the wilderness, but all Sullivan could think about was what he wouldn't give to hear that sound again.

She shifted against him, wrapping her leg around him as though she sensed he was trying to escape. What the—

The breath Sullivan had been holding crushed

from his lungs. He settled back where he'd been, pressed right against her, his front to her back. "You're awake, aren't you?"

Rolling into him, Jane startled him with a wide, gut-clenching grin. The dark, sultry look of her gaze constricted his throat, and a shiver chased down his spine. Her pupils expanded. For an instant, he swore he saw desire blazing in her eyes. Or maybe the hypothermia had done more damage to his brain than he'd originally thought. "I couldn't wait to see your reaction when you woke up and found a naked woman under the blanket with you. Surprise."

"Did I meet your expectations?" Sullivan was proud of the fact his voice sounded steady and calm. Especially considering how very far from calm he felt at the moment. Aware of how naked he was and how she couldn't possibly miss the show going on at her lower back, he held his weight away from her.

"Absolutely priceless. And, as a bonus, I got to see you naked." That amused smile of hers did funny things to his stomach, and he couldn't help but clench the blanket in his grip for some piece of control. Resting her hand on his chest, Jane pushed herself up to a sitting position, taking the blanket with her as she stood. Cool air rushed down his body, prickling his skin along the way. "Don't worry, big guy. It wasn't anything sexual. You were dying and I had to get your body temperature up."

Her long legs peeked out from between the folds of the blanket as she walked, the fire glinting off her bright red toenail polish. Not exactly the color he'd visualized for the woman he'd blamed for his brother's suicide this past year. Black maybe, something to match her soul.

But Jane had saved his life out there. Even if she was only using him to track down her stalker, that counted for something in his world. Her reputation said she was the JAG Corps prosecutor willing to do anything and everything to convict the men and women who interrupted her crusade for justice. He scanned over his clothing hanging from the rafters. The Full Metal Bitch had only kept him alive to fix her stalker problem. Nothing more.

There was a lot he didn't know about her, even more he couldn't trust. One thing he did know? He would've died out there today if it hadn't been for Jane. So, for now, he would choose to see a woman in danger, a woman who'd lost her grip on everything she thought she could control. Not someone who could turn on him at any moment.

She smiled over her shoulder at him as she

pulled her clothing from the makeshift laundry lines.

Pulling a pillow from the couch across his hips, Sullivan cleared his throat. "Thank you for saving my life out there. Can't imagine what it took to get me through that door. Couldn't have been easy."

"Guess that makes us even, doesn't it?" Her hair flipped around her head as she headed straight for the single bathroom on the other side of the cabin and shut the door tight. The sound of the lock clicking into place shut down any hint of something between them.

It wasn't going to happen. Not now. Not ever. She might've saved his life out there a few hours ago, but Jane had a lifetime of steel running through her veins, steel that'd gotten his brother killed. She was the reason he didn't have any family left in this world. Besides, she was a client, and Blackhawk Security operatives were never to get involved with their clients. No exceptions.

Which reminded him—he had to fill his team in on their new case. Because even without blackmail hanging over his head, the bastard terrorizing Jane owed Sullivan a new SUV.

He tossed the pillow back onto the couch and dressed in a hurry. She'd hung his clothes up by the fire to dry them out, and the warm fabric chased away the chill of Jane leaving his side. How could he have been so stupid out there? Rule number one when in below-freezing temperatures: stay dry, stay warm. He usually had enough sense to slow down and ensure he wasn't sweating. What had changed?

The bathroom door clicked open and his attention slid toward Jane as she stepped back into the main room. He pulled his shoulders back. There stood his answer. He hadn't exactly been in the right frame of mind after nearly getting run down by a tow truck. He'd wanted to get Jane to safety as fast as possible. Stupid. She'd proved she could take care of herself, had even saved his life in the process. Aside from a few bumps and bruises, she was no worse for wear.

"This is a nice place." She scanned over the small cabin, fingers stuffed into her jacket as he opened one drawer of his massive desk. "Not great security, though. A key taped to a bush? Thought you security consultants were better than that."

"Sometimes there's beauty in simplicity. Anybody breaking in here would expect some kind of elaborate security system, all the while wasting time looking for it. Gives me time to counter." Another one of those debilitating smiles overwhelmed her features, and he couldn't help but smile back. Sullivan flipped one of the many burner cell phones he'd unearthed from the desk over in his hand. The sensation of lightness disappeared, however, the longer he studied her. Eyes narrowing, he tried justifying the last few hours since she'd broken into his office. Why him? Why now? "What are you doing here, Jane?"

A small burst of laughter escaped from between those rosy lips. She motioned toward the front door. "Well, I couldn't very well leave you here alone after—"

"No." Sullivan closed in on her, the hairs on the back of his neck standing on end. "I mean why did you break into my office tonight? You had other options. Any number of bodyguards or private investigators in Anchorage would've jumped to help you for the right price. After all, you were ready to offer me anything." He halted no more than a foot from her, reading those deep hazel eyes for any sign of hesitation. "Why come to me?"

"Isn't it obvious?" She tried backing away but hit the wall beside the front door. "I had dirt on you and your family, and I knew I could use it to force you to help me. Saved myself a hell of a lot of money in the process."

Heat prickled under Sullivan's skin, crawling up his neck and warming his face. Only Jane crossed her arms across her chest and the strong pulse at the base of her neck beat unevenly. She didn't believe a word she was saying. And, thinking about it now, she'd only pulled the blackmail card when he'd refused to help her the first two times she'd asked. "You're lying."

Color left her features, a telling reaction he'd noted back in his office. Jane curled her fingers into the palms of her hands, stance wide as though she intended to run straight out the front door. Nervousness? Embarrassment? Difficult to tell when she wiped any kind of emotion from her features so fast.

"What do you want from me?" He stalked toward her. No. She wasn't going to hide behind that hardened exterior this time.

"I guess after what happened on the road, you deserve the truth. It seems stupid now, but I didn't have anyone else I could trust." She licked her bottom lip, but Sullivan refused to let the motion distract him this time. Answers. That was all he wanted. He'd risked his life—twice—for her. Now he needed to know why she'd pulled him into this mess. She cocked her head to the side. "I came to you because I saw how protective and dedicated you were to

Marrok during his trial. And after I uncovered that photo in my phone yesterday, I needed a little bit of that in my life." Raising that beautiful gaze to his, she let her shoulders deflate and she exhaled hard. "I needed *you*."

"I NEED TO brief my team." His gravelly voice played havoc with her insides, but Sullivan turned away from her, phone in hand. Refused to even look at her.

Every nerve in Jane's body caught fire. That was all he had to say? Watching him, she noted the strain around his eyes, the slightly haggard expression on his features as he spoke into the phone in whispered, clipped responses. She was used to it. In their line of work, she'd learned anybody could be listening in. Phone taps, parabolic mics. Without an idea of who her stalker was, why they'd come after her or what resources they had access to, she and Sullivan couldn't afford to be careless.

She headed into the kitchen. When had she eaten last? Her stomach rumbled. Too long ago. Sullivan turned toward her at the sound. The weight of his gaze slid across her sternum. Head down, she focused on her hunt for anything edible in this place. No luck. He obviously didn't stay here often. The walls were bare, the counters covered in dust. She ran her fingers over the cream granite, but ripped her hand away at the low temperature.

"I sent my forensic investigator, Vincent, to your place with some backup." Sullivan tossed the cell phone he'd been using onto the granite. Exhaustion played across his features, darkening the circles under his eyes. He hadn't gotten much sleep after nearly dying. Neither of them had, but Jane was too wound up and too anxious to figure this mess out. "If your stalker has been there, Vincent will find the evidence and call me back. Could be an hour, could be tomorrow. Just depends."

"Okay. What do we do until then?" She couldn't sit around waiting for some maniac to make the next move. There had to be something in her case files, something in her work for the army that could point them in the right direction to an ID of who'd T-boned them back at the bridge.

"We dig into your cases." Sullivan slid onto the bar stool on the other side of the granite countertop as though using it as a barrier between them. Probably a good idea. Because those heated, confusing minutes of them under the blanket in front of the fire together hadn't exactly gone as Jane had expected. His skin had pressed against hers from chest to toes, his very prominent arousal at her lower back, and the way he'd feathered his fingertips over her shoulder... Jane swallowed back the memories. His touch had felt good, real. Then again, she'd lived the past few months as a hermit and wouldn't know the difference between her own arousal and the simple need for human contact. Jane shivered. No. That wasn't it. She'd recognized the difference. She just hadn't felt that kind of drowning heat in a long time. Her insides burned to close the distance between them for another passing glimpse of it, however fleeting.

But Sullivan's reaction had been simple biology. There'd been a naked woman pressed against him and his body had responded. He didn't want her. Because no matter how many heated moments they shared, how many times they laughed together or how long they talked, Sullivan blamed her for his brother's suicide. Plain and simple.

"I'm already having the files brought from your town house by another operative on my team," he said.

Pressure built behind her sternum. Sullivan might not use all of his training from his military days for Blackhawk Security, but from what she'd read of him, he never missed a clue. She cleared her throat, stuffing her hands into her sweatshirt pockets. "Good idea. I've already gone through most of them, but another set of eyes might uncover something I missed."

Jane's stomach growled again.

"You need to eat and rest before Elliot gets here with the files." Sullivan stood, his wide shoulders blocking her view of the living room and the fire popping and cracking in the fireplace. Muscles flexed across his chest and arms, and Jane swallowed the rush of saliva filling her mouth. "I don't come up here often so I'm sorry to say there's nothing more than a few MREs lying around, but there should be enough in the duffel bags we brought to last us three days." He searched the living room. "Where did you put the bags after I tried to kill myself out there? I'll make us something to eat."

Jane's responding smile to his willingness to feed her disappeared. Exhaling, she ran her hand through her hair. Crap. "I left them outside. I wasn't thinking after I pulled you in—"

"Don't worry about it." He stepped right into her, that massive chest of his brushing against her. Staring down at her, Sullivan bent at the knees to look her right in the eye, his hands posed above her arms as though he didn't dare touch her. And she didn't blame him. The difference in height between them was laughable, but she appreciated the even ground now. His hands rested around her upper arms. Her insides flipped as his body heat spread through her, but she didn't pull away. "You had your priorities straight. You saved my life. I'll get them. About how far did you drop them?"

Good. He'd just go get them. Her breathing eased the longer he kept his grip on her, but it took a few seconds to clear her head of his proximity enough to answer. "Beyond the tree line. I don't think it snowed enough to cover my tracks. You should be able to follow them to the bags."

"All right. And when I get back, we'll call Anchorage PD to have them put an APB out for that tow truck." He dropped his hold on her, spinning toward his discarded gear drying over the fireplacc. A shiver rushed through her, but Jane held her ground as Sullivan donned his shoulder holster and thick coat. He reached under the built-in desk where the keyboard drawer clicked into place and removed a Glock, disengaged the magazine and pulled back the slide to check the chamber. He moved in quick, confident steps to reload the magazine and put a round in the chamber as though he'd done the same moves a thousand times before. Which he probably had. "I shouldn't be gone more than five minutes." He checked the batteries in the flashlight next. "If anything happens while I'm out there, use the burner phone to call the last number I dialed. It'll put you directly through to my guy Elliot. He's the closest right now, and he'll get here as fast as he can."

Jane nodded. He wouldn't be gone more than a few minutes, but she pointed toward the gun. "Do you have an extra one of those for me? Just in case." They'd already proved anything could happen. For crying out loud, a tow truck had blindsided them on purpose. She wasn't about to make it easier for this psychopath to get to her.

A smile lit up his features before he turned toward what she assumed was the only bedroom in the cabin. Mere seconds later, he handed her another Glock. "This is my service weapon from the SEALs and my favorite gun. If you have to shoot it outside for any reason, make sure there's no snow in the barrel and that you've warmed it up. Otherwise, it might blow up in your hands."

"I went through weapons training, too, remember? I know how to handle my guns in cold weather." Jane hit the button to disengage the magazine and pulled back the slide to clear the chamber, just as Sullivan had done with his own gun. Faster than she thought possible, the guarded curiosity in Sullivan's eyes changed to something dark, primal. She clenched her lower abdomen. Air stalled in her throat. She focused on the gun in her hand. "Besides, you won't be gone that long. I'm sure I can manage to take care of myself for five minutes."

"Of that—" he secured the Glock he'd taken from under the desk in his shoulder holster, eyes scanning her from head to toe "—I have no doubt." Sullivan disappeared out the door without looking back.

The goose bumps along her forearms receded the longer Jane stared after him. There was no denying it now. She'd seen the way he'd looked at her, the way he'd held on to her earlier. He wanted the intel she'd called in a few favors to get, the one with his real identity inside. Because there was no way that man wanted her for any other reason. No matter how deep he'd buried his past, she'd uncovered the truth and she'd known the second she confronted him with it, she would pay for using blackmail. What was he going to do? Torture her with desire until she gave him everything she had on him and his family?

Jane leaned against the countertop, Sullivan's service weapon comfortable in her grip. Now that she thought about it, torture by desire was one of the better ways to go. Especially with a six-foot-four, muscled, powerfully built SEAL. A smile pulled at her lips. Crap, she imagined that outcome between them all too easily. The heat, the explosion of passion, the—

The front door slammed open and her muscle memory hefted the gun up. She aimed, ready to pull the trigger. Adrenaline pumped fast through her veins as Sullivan swung his head around the thick, wooden door. Jane dropped the gun to her side, heart beating a mile a second. She could've shot him. "You scared me to death. Do you always barge into a room like that?"

Sullivan stomped his boots on the mat at the door, then headed straight for the burner phone on the kitchen counter. He brushed against her, but instead of heat penetrating through her jacket like before, she only felt cold. Something was wrong. Stabbing the pad of his thumb into the keypad, he brought the phone up to his ear, those sea-blue eyes glued on her. Darkness etched into his expression, and Jane took a step back to give him some space. "The bags are gone."

## Chapter Four

The guns, extra ammunition, food, tracks, everything was gone. Looked like Jane's mysterious stalker had tracked her back here after all. The phone rang once in his ear before Elliot Dunham, his private investigator, picked up.

"Go for Dunham," Elliot said.

Sullivan checked his watch. "How far out are you?"

"Five minutes."

"Make it three. The bastard knows we're here."

"See you in two." The revving of a car engine echoed in the background before the line disconnected. As an operative on the Blackhawk Security team, Elliot would understand to come in hot—armed and ready for a fight. Sullivan had swiped the private investigator off the Iraqi streets right after Sullivan's discharge from the SEALs. The man had a knack for finding and recovering classified documents, digging into a person's life, discovering those secrets his target didn't want the world to know about. Like a pit bull with his favorite chew toy, Elliot never gave up and never surrendered. Most likely a side effect of his con artist days; each case a long con. With a genius-level IQ, he dug deep, he got personal. At least until the job was done. Then he disappeared to start fresh. It hadn't been difficult to recruit him either. Only a few phone calls that could put Elliot back into an Iraqi jail cell.

His next call was to Anchorage PD to report the tow truck that'd nearly rammed them into the Gulf of Alaska. A minute later, Sullivan tossed the phone onto the counter and rubbed at his face.

"Is Elliot bringing supplies?" Jane stared up at him, arms wrapped around her small midsection. Her shoulders hunched inward as though she felt the weight of someone watching her. Which Sullivan bet was familiar by now.

The same weight pressed in on him, too, but they only had to wait a few more minutes. Then they could get through her case files and find out who exactly had turned Jane into a target. After that, they'd come up with a plan. "I make every member of my team carry extra guns, ammo and food in case of emergency."

"Do you think whoever is after me is out there, right now, watching us?" Jane's voice trembled. She was scared. And rightfully so.

Whoever had taken their bags had wiped any evidence of their existence from the snow. There weren't a whole lot of men who possessed that kind of skill, Sullivan being one of the few. His father had ensured his sons knew how to hunt their prey properly, before the old man had turned into the sick psychopath he became known for. But right now, in this moment, Sullivan wasn't the hunter. He felt like the prey.

A soft ringing reached his ears, and Jane extracted her cell phone from her jacket pocket. Frowning, she put the phone to her ear. "Hello?"

He couldn't hear the response from this distance and, while eavesdropping on his client's phone calls was technically part of the job, Sullivan wouldn't crowd her. *I needed you.* Those three small words had been circling his brain since they'd left her mouth.

"Who is this?" The color drained from Jane's features.

Sullivan's instincts prickled at the alarm in her voice. He stepped into her personal space, forcing her to meet his gaze, then reached for her phone. He hit the speaker button, holding the phone between them. "Who the hell is this?"

"He can't protect you, Jane," the voice whispered across the line. Her name on the bastard's lips tightened the muscles down Sullivan's spine. "You're going to pay for what you've done."

Memorizing the number on the screen, Sullivan gripped the phone tighter. He couldn't peg an accent due to the whispering, no dialect to pinpoint where her stalker originated from. "Come within three hundred feet of her and I will tear you apart. You tried to kill her once. Won't happen again. Understand?" His voice dropped low—deadly—as he studied the fear skating across Jane's features. "Don't call this number again."

He moved to hang up the call.

"Always the protector... *Sullivan*." Laughter trickled through the phone.

Sullivan's thumb froze over the end button. A shiver spread across his shoulders. The line went dead, only static and crackling from the fireplace filling the silence.

In a split second, one of the burner phones he kept on hand was at his ear, ringing through to Blackhawk Security's head of network security. The line picked up. "Elizabeth, trace this number." He recited the number he'd memorized from the call. "I want a location as soon as possible. Send it straight to the number I'm calling you from."

"You got it, boss," the former NSA analyst said.

He hung up. Sullivan's gaze lifted from the phone as Jane backed away. The terror etched into her expression urged him toward her. Without hesitation, he reached for her. "Jane…"

Eyes wide, mouth slack, she shut down her expression, and Sullivan dropped his hand. "He's here. He's *watching* me. He knows you're with me."

That had always been a possibility. Stalkers liked to keep tabs on their targets. The bastard had most likely been the one responsible for taking their gear, too. She'd known the risks going into this, but Sullivan wouldn't remind her of them now. In this moment, he needed her head on straight. Focused. "You hired me because I'm good at my job. He's never going to get close to you. You have my word."

"Thank you." Her chin notched higher. Jane shifted her weight onto her toes as though she intended to kiss him, and right then, all too easily, Sullivan imagined how it'd feel to claim that perfect mouth of hers. Would she taste as good as she smelled? Damn it. Why couldn't he keep himself in check around her?

Three knocks on the door ripped him back. The thick wood swung inward, and Sullivan shoved Jane behind him. Her fingers clenched the back of his shirt as he unholstered the Glock at his side. The man hunting Jane most likely wouldn't knock, but maybe there were polite stalkers out there in the world.

"And here I thought I'd get to shoot someone when I got here." Elliot Dunham's wide grin shifted the dark stubble across his jawline. The lines at the edges of his stormy gray eyes deepened. The private investigator holstered his own weapon underneath a thick cargo jacket and kicked the door closed behind him. "Good news for everyone. The perimeter is clear, and I won't get blood on my new shirt."

"We wouldn't want that. I'd have to hear about it all night." Sullivan couldn't help but smile as he clapped Elliot on the back. "Did you bring the files?"

"Got them in the truck along with extra munitions and snacks. But I have to be honest, I ate all the nuts on the way here. This place is in the middle of nowhere." Swiveling his head around Sullivan, Elliot caught sight of their new client. Jane. The con-man-turned-investigator side-stepped his boss, something close to intrigue smoothing out his features. "And you must be Jane. Your picture doesn't do you justice."

"You're kidding, right?" Jane asked. "*That's* your opening line?"

"Oh, I like her." Elliot's smile made another appearance.

Sullivan clamped a hand on his investigator's shoulder. Elliot had absolutely no interest in their new client, but something inside had tightened at the thought of another man coming anywhere near her with that look on his face. What did he care? He'd taken her on as a client, however forced. He didn't have any kind of claim on her. "How about you do your job and get me those files from the truck?"

"Sure thing, boss." Elliot half saluted Jane, then spun back toward the front door and disappeared.

A tri-chimed message tone brought the burner phone back into his hand. Sullivan read Elizabeth's message, then dropped the phone onto the hardwood and stomped on it. The screen cracked under his boots, pieces of plastic skating across the floor. "My team couldn't trace the number. We weren't on the line long enough to get a location."

"And you felt the need to take it out on your phone?" she asked.

"Can't be too careful." In reality, he'd been thinking ahead. If this case went south and the man hunting Jane expanded his crosshairs, Sullivan wouldn't leave any evidence behind that could lead to his team.

"So that's your private investigator." Not a question. Jane's arm brushed his as she passed him heading into the living room. A shot of awareness trailed up Sullivan's arm. He slapped a hand over the oversensitized skin, but she didn't notice. Head in the game. Standing in front of the fire, her bruises and cuts illuminated by the brilliant orange flames, Jane still held her head high. There was a target on her back, but she hadn't fallen apart. She didn't trust him with her emotions. Didn't seem to trust anyone.

"Elliot is the best private investigator in the country." He closed in on her one step at a time, giving in to the urge to have her nearby in case her stalker took a shot through the front windows. He'd already tried to kill her once. No telling what he'd do next. At least for now. "Used to be a con man. Elliot can read people. He has the resources to dig into their lives and a genius-level IQ to see three steps ahead. He'll find whoever's targeting you."

"What if he can't?" Turning toward him, Jane gave him an exhausted smile. Her shoulders sagged as though she'd collapse into a puddle on the floor. "I've been through those files a dozen times. I know them better than anyone, and I couldn't pick out any potential suspects." She massaged her temples with her fingers. "I just want my life back."

"Look at me." Sullivan closed the small space between them. He pushed every ounce of sincerity into his expression, his gaze, his voice, but didn't move to touch her this time. "I don't give my word lightly. You might've blackmailed me into it, but I promised to protect you, and I will." The small muscles in his jaw tightened. "We will figure this out."

She nodded. "I believe you."

"Good." Four hours ago, he'd tried kicking her out of his office. But now... They were in this together. He'd saved her life. She'd saved his. And he wouldn't let some nutjob with a sick obsession get close to her again. No matter how much he blamed her for Marrok's death. "You're dead on your feet. Why don't you go lie down in the bedroom? I'll wake you if we find a lead."

Jane nodded, her eyes brighter than a few

moments ago. "I'll also expect that meal you promised when I come out."

A laugh rumbled through his chest as Sullivan watched her disappear into the bedroom. Flashes of those long legs peeking out from under his blanket skittered across his mind, and his gut warmed. He stared after her a few seconds longer, but the weight of being watched pressed between his shoulder blades. His neck heated. *Damn.* "How long have you been standing there?"

"Long enough to see you're going to break your own rule if you're not careful." Elliot dropped the box of Jane's case files and laptop onto the built-in desk and raised his hands in surrender. "Okay, now you look like you want to kill me."

No way was he going to talk about this with his private investigator. Or anybody. Ever. "What did you find when you went through the files?"

"I've narrowed it down to two possibilities within the army after you said the guy erased his tracks after taking off with your supplies. That takes a lot of skill, and not many of the people she has regular contact with have any kind of training like that." Elliot shoved the lid off the box and extracted three manila file folders. "Your girl took some damn fine notes on the cases she worked. Made my job easier."

His girl? Not even close. But Sullivan didn't correct his investigator. He took the files from Elliot and scanned over the extensive notes inside. Must've been Jane's handwriting. Precise, to the point. Nothing fancy. But the purple and pink Post-its stuck through the files surprised him. Just as her red toenail polish had. He scanned over the first file. "Staff Sergeant Marrok Warren."

Something sour swept across his tongue.

"Now, that guy is a piece of work. There's only one problem." Elliot leveraged his weight against the desk and crossed his arms over his chest. "Jane prosecuted him for sexual assault of three female enlisted soldiers, but—"

"He's dead." There it was. Stamped across Jane's case file in big red letters. *Deceased.* Sullivan's ears rang. He discarded the file back into the box, his body strung as tight as a tension spring. His brother might've had the skills to pull off blindsiding them in the SUV and taking their supplies without leaving behind a trace, but it wasn't possible. Marrok Warren was dead. Sullivan had buried him ten months ago almost to the day.

"That would be the problem. I tied him to

Jane's case because of the guy's father." Elliot pulled a bag of peanuts from his jacket pocket. "Ever heard of the Anchorage Lumberjack? Killed twelve victims, all with an ax. With Staff Sergeant Warren dead, could be a close family member coming after Jane now, maybe one of those psychopathic groupies I'm always hearing about. Wonder what they're like…"

Sullivan crumpled the files in his hand, the tendons in his neck straining. He locked his attention on Elliot, then took a deep breath, forcing himself to relax. "Who else do you have?"

"We've got her commanding officer." His private investigator nodded toward the second file in Sullivan's hand, ignoring the obvious tension that'd filled the room. "Major Patrick Barnes is Jane's CO. He'd know her daily schedule, her routine, and have access to all of her files. He would know her whereabouts while on tour, and he's the one who grants permission for her to go on leave."

"It's not Major Barnes," a familiar voice said.

Twisting around, Sullivan locked on to Jane, the grip around his rib cage lightening at the sight of her. As long as she was in his sights, she was safe. He tossed the files onto the desk. "You should be resting."

"Couldn't wind down. Besides, this is my

case. I should be helping." Jane shoved off from against the doorjamb and sauntered forward. Reaching for Major Barnes's file, she scanned through the pages, her proximity setting Sullivan's nerve endings on high alert. She tossed the file on top of Marrok Warren's and crossed her arms over her chest. "I owe Barnes my life. He tackled me to the ground after an IED exploded in the parking lot outside my office in Afghanistan two months ago. He wouldn't have done that just to turn around and come after me himself. And he has no motive."

"All right. Then we take a tour of your life outside the army. The only other name that stands out to me is Christopher Menas." Elliot handed the file to Jane, but shifted his gaze to Sullivan before settling back against the desk. Hesitant? "He's won a few hunting awards, but that's about all I know aside from his criminal record. I can't find any employment records, no college degree, no military record, nothing that says he's changed his name, or a death certificate attached to this guy. Menas simply dropped off the grid after skipping bail, but you two had a complicated past and that's why I'm pinning him as a suspect."

"I can't believe this." She stared at the name on the edge of the folder, her eyes panicked and wide. She slipped her index finger between the yellow card stock but didn't move to open the file. "I haven't thought about Christopher in years."

"Jane?" Warning bells rang in Sullivan's head as he closed in on her. "What are you thinking?"

Tearing her attention from the folder, Jane lifted her gaze to his. "It's him. He's the one doing this to me."

CHRISTOPHER MENAS.

Flashes of his face, of those cold brown eyes and dark skin, lit up the back of her eyelids. Jane bolted upright off the bed, out of breath, surrounded by pure darkness. She'd been in love—outright smitten—with the quarterback of the University of Washington Huskies football team. And it'd all been a lie.

She couldn't see anything with the bedroom door shut, but her instincts screamed she wasn't alone. The silhouette of a man shifted in her peripheral vision. She slipped her hand under her pillow, curling her fingers around the gun Sullivan had lent her when she'd gone to bed.

"I'm not armed." A chair creaked to her left before the mattress dipped with added weight. Her hand relaxed from around the Glock. Sullivan. The light on the nightstand flickered to life, bathing his stern features in warmth. "Tell me about Christopher Menas."

"What?" She squinted into the brightness. "What time is it?"

"Just before dawn. You were talking in your sleep earlier. About Christopher Menas." Every muscle in her body tightened at that name. Sullivan's voice remained soft, coaxing. "I read the police report on him. He sexually assaulted two women while you two were dating. Your roommates, right? Right before he came after you."

A shiver chased up her spine. How could this be happening again? She'd moved on with her life, joined the army, made something of herself. She'd left that part of her life—left Christopher and everything that reminded her of him—behind.

"Is that why you went after my brother so aggressively? To make Marrok pay because your college boyfriend got away with his crimes?" Sullivan stared at her, stone-like. The muscles in his jawline flexed as though he was grinding his back molars, but Jane still forced herself to meet his gaze.

"Are you really accusing me of corruption, or is this because I prosecuted your brother for sexual assault?" She regretted the words the second they left her mouth. Clenching the sheets, she steadied her nerves. No. This was his job; this was why she'd blackmailed him in the first place. He got the job done, no matter what it took. And if Christopher was the man behind this, she'd make sure her ex paid this time. With Sullivan's help. "I'll tell you anything you need to know about Christopher, but believe me when I say this has nothing to do with you or your brother."

"How can I trust you?" Sullivan's calm, collected exterior broke around his eyes and mouth. "You charged my brother with these exact same crimes, which led to Marrok committing suicide. You're blackmailing me into helping you now. And you purposefully left out a credible lead."

*What?* "I never—"

"You told me you didn't have any ex-boyfriends who would hold a grudge against you. You're the one who turned Menas over to the police all those years ago. You knew he'd skipped bail. All this time you didn't think he was the one who might be after you?" Standing, Sullivan ran his hands through his hair. Shadows threw his features into sharper angles and brought out the darkness he'd kept under control up until now. "Damn it, Jane. I could've gotten people on him the second we left my office and none of this would've happened."

"How do you know it's him stalking me or he's the one who ran us off the road? You said it yourself, whoever took the bags didn't leave any evidence, and you never got a look at the driver." Jane threw her legs over the edge of the bed and stood, thankful she'd chosen warmer attire tonight rather than her usual T-shirt and panties. None of this made sense. Why would her ex-boyfriend come after her now? That was a lifetime ago. The statute of limitations had run out on his charges and he'd never gone to prison. What could he possibly hold against her now?

"Weren't you the one who said, 'It's him. He's the one doing this to me,' out there?" Dropping his hands, Sullivan faced her head-on, body still tense.

She didn't know how to respond. The idea of Christopher coming back into her life after all this time...

"Anchorage PD recovered the vehicle. The tow truck that blindsided us was recovered from behind a gas station just inside town." Sullivan pulled a hand through his short hair. "My forensics guy has been working with Anchorage PD. They've confirmed the black paint on the fender is from my SUV. Jane, the registration is filed under Christopher Menas's name."

The air in her throat froze. They had a lead, proof. Christopher had come to Anchorage. For her. Locking her teeth together, Jane tugged her sweatshirt off the edge of the bed, then shoved her feet into her boots. She'd gone into the army because of her ex, learned to protect herself against men like him. But no more running. Christopher wanted revenge? He was going to have to work for it. Heading for the door, she gave into the sudden rush of determination pumping through her. "Then what are we waiting for? Let's go."

"Go where?" he asked.

Wasn't this man a SEAL, trained to think two steps ahead of everybody else to get the upper hand in any situation? "To Christopher's. He must have a safe house, a hotel room or an apartment—something around here if he's stalking me, right?"

"We can't go barging into the man's private residence, Jane." Sullivan shot to his feet and wrapped his hand around her arm, but she wrenched away. He seemed to be doing a lot of that in the last twenty-four hours, touching her, but now wasn't the time to analyze the contact. Despite the fact he'd accused her of corruption, they had a stalker to find. "We're not the police. We don't have a warrant. The best thing we can do is put surveillance on him for the next couple days. Then we can go from there."

On any other case, she'd agree. She'd taken an oath as a lawyer. She was supposed to play by the book, but this case had turned more personal than she'd imagined. "I don't have a couple of days. I need my life back *now*." Throwing the door open, she stalked straight toward Elliot, who was asleep on the couch. "I need your car keys."

Elliot's feet lifted off the couch as he dropped his arms away from his forehead. A yawn twisted his features as he rubbed sleep from his eyes. "Well, good morning to you, too."

"Keys." Jane extended her hand. "Please."

"I take it you told her about the tow truck," Elliot said to Sullivan over her shoulder. He sat up, digging into his jacket pocket before dangling the car keys in front of her. "Have a nice field trip, sweetheart. Call me if you need me."

She swiped the keys from his hand.

"If we're going—" Sullivan fisted both his hands in Elliot's jacket and hefted him from the couch "—then you're coming, too."

"We don't have much time. Christopher is smart. He probably left that truck there for us to trace back to him, but I doubt he's going to stick around and risk arrest." Jane took a deep breath to clear her head and handed the keys back to Elliot. A rush of cold air slammed against her as they stepped back into the freezing Alaskan wilderness. It took a few seconds for her lungs to catch up with the change in temperature, but she refused to slow down. They had to catch Christopher by surprise, but the sun would be up soon and they'd lose their cover of night.

Once they were all within the safety of the truck, Elliot put the shifter into Reverse but didn't move. "What exactly is our plan here?"

"You're a private investigator. I assume you already know where Christopher is hiding." Jane buckled herself into the back seat. "I want to surprise him and get some answers. That's the plan for right now."

"And if he's armed?" Sullivan turned around, his gaze glued to her.

"Isn't that why I hired you?" Throwing his own words back in his face wouldn't smooth the tension between them, but Jane still couldn't believe he'd implied she'd had anything personal against his brother during the court-martial. Sure, Marrok's charges were nearly identical to Christopher Menas's, but she'd always strived for compartmentalization and professionalism when prosecuting a case. She couldn't practice law if her emotions got the best of her. Hence that damn nickname. No emotion. No attachment. Jane cringed inwardly and crossed her arms over her chest as they pulled away from the cabin. But that wasn't her. Not anymore.

The truck barreled through the snow as they headed back toward Anchorage without signs of an ambush, but Jane still kept an eye out for any rogue tow trucks waiting for them at signals through town. According to Elliot's research, Christopher Menas had been renting an apartment near Taku Lake. Within twenty minutes, the private investigator parked the pickup two blocks from their destination.

The apartment complex wasn't anything special—two levels, blond-wood balconies with white stucco on the sides. Trees and shrubs gave the complex a lighter feel, but as Jane stepped onto the pavement, a ball of dread fisted at the base of her spine.

"He's in apartment 310." Sullivan stayed on her tail as she headed down the street and for the third building to her right. Dressed for warmer temperatures, he showed off long lengths of muscle down his arms, and the flood of apprehension gripping her disappeared. "May I remind you this isn't a good idea? We have no idea what's waiting for us on the other side of that door."

Right then, she didn't care. "I'm putting an end to this. For good."

Screeching metal filled Jane's ears as Elliot extracted a long steel tube from the bed of his truck. Both Sullivan and Jane spun, staring at him. "What?" He hefted the small battering ram over his shoulder. "It's in case we want to commit a felony."

The breath she'd been holding rushed from her. She couldn't believe any of this. She hadn't thought of Christopher Menas in years. But here she was, climbing up the steps to her ex-boyfriend's apartment to find out why he was trying to kill her.

Sullivan maneuvered in front of her, using his body to shield her from the door. Her throat tightened as his fingers smoothed over her jacket. He couldn't have meant what he'd said back at the cabin, could he? After everything they'd been through the last twenty-four hours, he couldn't think so low of her. She'd saved his life. Didn't that count for something? Pounding on the door, Sullivan stepped back and pulled his weapon. As did Elliot with his free hand.

No answer. No sounds of movement inside. It was barely sunrise. Surely her stalker could have had the decency to be home when she came to confront him.

Sullivan pounded his fist against the wood again. Nothing. "Are you sure you want to do this?" He nodded toward Menas's front door. "We can still go back, come at this from another angle."

Go back? She couldn't go back. She couldn't walk away now. Jane swallowed the hesitation screaming at the back of her mind. "I'm sure."

"All right. Breaking and entering it is, Counselor. Just promise not to charge us, since you're the one giving the orders." He stepped aside, ushering Elliot forward. "Have at it."

"Once we're in, be sure not to touch anything. Someone's about to call the police." Elliot slammed the head of the battering ram into the thick wood, and the door frame splintered. He hit it a second time, buckling the hinges, and within a minute, they were inside.

"Let's go. We don't have long before the police or a curious neighbor show up." Sullivan stepped inside first, Glock in his hand, body tense. Like the good security consultant she'd blackmailed him to be.

Jane's insides clenched as she followed close behind him. Whether it was from their conversation back in the bedroom or the situation, she couldn't tell. She hadn't seen Christopher Menas in nearly a decade.

Sullivan flipped on the lights with his elbow, and Jane leveraged her weight against one wall to clear her head. The inside of the apartment was…normal. No foul-smelling decaying bodies, no bloodstained carpets. The two-bedroom apartment had been decorated in a Southwestern theme—where Christopher was from—and looked like it'd been that way for a while. No quick getaway for him. Their suspect intended to stick around.

"Are you sure we have the right information?" Jane smoothed the hem of her coat sleeve over the back of the black leather couch. "This place doesn't exactly scream psychopath."

Searching the kitchen, Sullivan used a napkin to open drawers, go through receipts and sift through photos. He held up a business card for her to see, as Elliot checked out the back bedrooms. "We're in the right place."

She took the card from him, not entirely stable on her own two feet. "Menas Towing. Why didn't that show up in Elliot's research?" Jane scanned the rest of the apartment, taking anything—everything—in. There had to be something here that pointed to Jane as a target. According to the profilers she'd worked with on dozens of cases for the army, stalkers usually kept mementos of their victims. Trophies. But from what Jane could see, they'd made a mistake. There was nothing here. So if Christopher wasn't her stalker, then who was? The only evidence they had to go on was the tow truck registered in his name. "Who would be stupid enough to hit us with their own truck?"

"Nobody." Sullivan locked those mesmerizing eyes on her for the first time since accusing her of corruption. Her heart rate skyrocketed when he looked at her like that, like a puzzle he needed to solve. "Unless we're supposed to be here. What about the voice on the call? Did it sound like Menas?"

"I couldn't tell from the way he was whispering. And it's been so long since I've talked to him, I'm not sure I could identify it as his anyway." She ran through Sullivan's words a second time and half turned toward him. "Do you think somebody is setting Christopher up?"

"Not likely." Elliot stepped back into the main room and hitched a thumb over his shoulder. "You need to see this."

"What did you find?" Jane sprinted after the private investigator, heart in her throat. Had he found the evidence? Found Christopher? The hallway passed in a blur as she hurried after

Elliot toward the back bedroom. She halted at the door frame. Her jaw slackened. She couldn't breathe. The world tilted on an axis, but she managed to stay upright.

"What the hell?" Sullivan's words echoed her own thoughts as he brushed past her and moved into the room.

Jane shook her head, clinging to the door frame with everything she had. "I don't think we're in the wrong place anymore."

## Chapter Five

No matter where he turned, Jane was there.

"There has to be hundreds of photos of me here." Jane's voice shook as she stepped up to one wall.

Something deep in his chest urged him to reach out for her, but Sullivan stood his ground. This wasn't the time. There were more photos than the one on Jane's phone of her sleeping. These showed her eating. In court. Right outside her home. His insides raged as he scanned over the closest wall a second time. In the shower. From the look of it, the past three months of her life had been documented in pictures taped to four plain white walls. Rage burned hot under his sternum. The sick freak had stolen precious moments from her life—too many to count—and Jane would never get them back.

She slid her fingertips over a handful of photos, seeming not to even breathe.

And he couldn't take staying away any longer. Sullivan took a step toward her, hand outstretched. "Jane—"

"This is my life. He…" Her lips parted on a strong inhale. She dropped her hand, turning toward him, and he froze. Swallowing, Jane covered her mouth. She rushed past him, her vanilla scent thick on the air. "I think I'm going to be sick."

She fled the room. A few seconds later, a door slammed down the hallway and he shut his eyes against the onslaught of surveillance her stalker had collected. One inhale. Two. The protector buried deep inside of him clawed its way to the surface for a breath of fresh air. Christopher Menas was a dead man. Whatever game the bastard had going on with Jane was over. Sullivan was coming for him. Opening his eyes, he spun toward the hallway. "Elliot, document everything. We're leaving."

He had to get Jane out of here. The police were most likely on their way from when Elliot had brought down the door. She couldn't get wrapped up in their investigation. The second the report went live, the army would limit her security clearance and she'd be at risk of losing her job. Stalking down the hall toward the bathroom, gun in hand, he listened for signs of movement. He was sure their suspect wasn't in the apartment, but a man who could cover his tracks in the Alaskan wilderness had to have a few more tricks up his sleeves. And Sullivan wasn't about to make a mistake on this case. Not with Jane's life on the line.

With three light taps on the bathroom door, he leaned against the wood. "Jane?"

No answer.

His heartbeat rocketed into his throat. He squeezed his free hand around the door handle, but didn't move to open it. Yet. Fanning his grip over the Glock, he scanned down the hallway. "Are you okay?"

Still nothing.

"All right." Backing up, Sullivan cradled the gun in both hands, prepared to kick in the door if he had to, to get to her. "I'm coming in."

The door swung open on silent hinges, and the torn woman in front of him hurried to swipe salty streaks of tears from her face with the back of her hand. In a split second, she locked her emotions away as though she hadn't fallen apart out of his sight. "I'm fine. I just needed a minute."

"You don't have to hide from me, Jane." His throat tightened, but he released his suffocating grip on the gun. Every cell in his body urged him to stand as a pillar of comfort for her, and he straightened. Forget the past. Forget the rules for a few seconds. Jane was falling apart and it was his job to hold his client's life together. Even if she'd blackmailed him into it. Closing in on her slowly, he brushed a stray tear from her face, careful to leave space for her to escape if she wanted. Hesitation shot down his arms and into his chest, but this time he didn't pull away. Didn't feel the need. Those hazel eyes closed as she leaned into him for support, and he set his chin onto the crown of her head. Her short black hair tumbled forward against his chest and his fingers tingled with the urge to shove it behind her ear so she'd look up at him. "I'm sorry you had to see all of that. You don't deserve this."

For the first time since Jane had broken into his office last night, he meant every word. Her body heat tunneled through his jacket, sinking into his muscles, his bones. The tension throughout his body relaxed second by second. All Sullivan could think about in this moment was taking her back to the cabin and shielding her from what was to come. Men willing to kill the object of their obsessions didn't give up easily. But she couldn't run. Not from this.

Sullivan inhaled deep. He smelled…smoke.

"Do you smell that?" Jane pulled back.

"Elliot." Panic wrapped a tight fist around his heart. Clamping his hand around hers, Sullivan tugged Jane after him down the hallway. After discovering Menas's sick collection, he wasn't about to let her out of his sight. Black smoke escaped out from under the second bedroom door. Had he closed it behind him? He dropped his hold on her and kicked in the door. Bright flames climbed up the walls where Jane's photos used to hang. Covering his face and eyes in the crook of his arm, Sullivan avoided the majority of the smoke but couldn't see anything worth a damn. There was too much smoke. Too many flames. "Elliot!"

"Sullivan, there!" Jane latched onto his arm, pointing to one corner of the room. Without waiting for him, she launched herself through the flames consuming the door frame.

"Jane, no!" He grabbed after her but missed her jacket by mere centimeters. She couldn't pull Elliot out of there on her own. Not with flames consuming the walls on every side. The roar of the fire drowned out any sounds of Jane or his private investigator. Lunging into the heart of the fire, he kept low, searching for her, searching for Elliot. "Jane!"

"Over here." A cough led him toward the back of the room. The crackling of the flames nearly drowned out her voice, but he homed in on the uncontrollable coughing coming from his right.

"Jane." Within seconds, he'd wrapped his hands around her arms and shoved her back toward the bedroom door. He covered his mouth and nose with the crook of his arm as smoke worked into his lungs. Squinting from the heat, he fought to see the door. "Get out of here. Get outside."

She'd found Elliot knocked out near the west wall. Hiking his private investigator over his shoulder, Sullivan narrowly avoided a falling rafter as he wound through debris and flames.

Outside, he breathed in as much clean air as his lungs allowed, nearly collapsing as his muscles weakened from oxygen depletion. Jane ran forward, eyes wide, hands outstretched to catch them both. The three of them fell in a pile of limbs and heavy breathing as sirens filled the night. In less than seven minutes, fire crews sprinted to put out the blaze. Staring up at the damage, Sullivan noted the entire building had caught fire.

"How many—" His lungs worked overtime to expel the smoke he'd inhaled. He didn't want to think about the casualties. There was no way the fire had been a coincidence. Christopher

Menas had known they were there. The fire had most likely been set to destroy the evidence he'd left behind. Maybe to hurt them, to hurt Jane.

"I got them all out." Jane cradled Elliot's head in her lap, her palms on both sides of his slackened jaw. "When you pushed me out the door, I pulled the fire alarm."

Streaks of soot lined her jaw and forehead, enhancing the bruises and scrapes from the car accident, but Jane had never been more beautiful than right in this moment. She'd charged into that bedroom to save one of his men's lives. And ended up saving many others in the building. What was it about the woman he blamed that compelled her to keep saving lives?

A nasty gash bled freely from the right side of Elliot's head. Knocked unconscious. Damn it. They'd walked straight into Menas's trap.

Sullivan shook his head. He couldn't breathe. Couldn't think. Until he saw the blood streaking down Jane's cargo jacket. Reaching across Elliot's unconscious body for her, he inspected the wound. "Are you okay?"

"Nothing a few stitches won't fix." She twisted her arm so she could see it better. "I'm kind of sad about this jacket, though. It's my favorite."

Squealing tires and red and blue lights claimed

his attention. He tightened his hold on Jane, unwilling to let her out of his sight yet. But that gash wouldn't stitch itself.

EMTs rushed to their side, hefting Elliot onto a stretcher and prying his eyes open. But not before Sullivan lifted Elliot's phone from his private investigator's jacket pocket. Elliot had documented Christopher Menas's collection in that bedroom, and the cops weren't about to stick it in some evidence room before Sullivan could review the photos. Evidence tampering be damned.

Elliot was in good hands. Sullivan's instincts said Menas wouldn't come after him. But Jane? That was another story. They couldn't stay here. Menas had been watching them. Could still be watching them. "Are you okay to move?"

"Would you throw me over your shoulder like you did with Elliot if I said no?" Lean muscle flexed down the backs of her thighs as she stood, and Sullivan fought a smile. "I'm fine. Really. And I'm glad those pictures didn't survive."

"You went in that bedroom for Elliot. Looks like I just might owe you again." Freezing gusts of wind beat against him on one side as he hiked himself to his feet, blistering heat from the burning apartment on the other. EMTs closed in on them, two leading Jane to an ambulance and another swinging a light in front of his face. He shoved the technician away. He was fine. Minor case of smoke inhalation. Nothing Sullivan hadn't lived through before. His breath sawed in and out of him as bright orange flames licked up the side of the apartment building.

They could've died in there.

Two Anchorage police units rolled up as Sullivan messaged his team from Elliot's phone. Keeping Jane in his peripheral vision as medics looked her over on the back of the ambulance, he headed toward the officers to give his statement. While Anchorage PD would run their own investigation, he had no intention of leaving Jane's case in their hands. They'd already failed to take her claim seriously. He had far more resources to bring this particular arsonist down.

Within five minutes, another Blackhawk Security SUV pulled into the scene. Sullivan caught sight of his weapons expert as the six-foot-five-inch wall of solid, sunglass-loving muscle stepped out onto the pavement. Anthony Harris surveyed the scene from behind his favorite pair of sunglasses, chest wide, fingers relaxed at his side. The thick beard covering the former Ranger's jawline hid his expression, but

Sullivan sensed he was calculating the chances of another attack and where it'd come from. Always ready for the fight, always on alert. That was what made Anthony one of the best men on the Blackhawk Security team. "Need a ride?"

"Jane." Sullivan pushed through the EMTs blocking his path to her and offered her his hand. "We're leaving." Her long fingers slid across his palm without hesitation, and he pulled her to her feet. They had to get her off the street. Most stalkers willing to take out their targets in daylight—in public—loved watching the aftermath of their work. She wasn't safe here, even with three EMTs and two Anchorage PD officers. But his team could protect her. *He* could protect her. "I've got you."

He wasn't sure where the words had come from, but Jane nodded once, setting his racing heart at ease. Hand wrapped tight around hers, he headed toward Anthony and the safety of the SUV. She'd been through hell—again—and he fought the urge to wrap her in his arms. Holding her back in that apartment, just before it'd burned to the ground, had comforted him as much as it had her. He'd overstepped the boundaries he'd set between them. Didn't seem as important then as it did now. Jane. She'd been all that'd mattered.

Shoving her into the back of the SUV, Sullivan climbed in after her. "Go," he ordered Anthony, and the SUV spun around before he shut the door.

"Where are we going? Christopher knew the tow truck would be recovered, and that we would come here." Voice soft, Jane swept her gaze across the back window, knuckles white from her grip on the edge of her seat. "He was waiting for us."

"We're going on lockdown. I've already called in the rest of my team to meet us." Sullivan studied the rooftops as they sped through downtown. Water kicked up along the side of the SUV, but he forced himself to keep his senses on the possible threat rather than the smell of smoke coming off her skin. Unholstering the Glock at his side, he cleared the chamber and loaded another round. Just in case. "Look on the bright side. You didn't have to drag anyone out of that building."

Jane's resulting laugh dissolved the knot of tightness behind his sternum, and it became easier to breathe. His smile vanished. This wasn't right. He shouldn't be trying to make her laugh, to help her cope with the situation. Shouldn't want to hike her into his side like he had some kind of claim.

"We're here." Anthony swung the SUV into Blackhawk Security's parking garage. The gate locked down behind them the second the bumper cleared. Four other vehicles had been parked close to the elevator doors. The rest of the team had already arrived and were waiting for orders. Good. The sooner he wrapped up Jane's case, the better. He might've led some of the blackest operations the US government had ever ordered during his time as a SEAL, but Sullivan only had so much control when it came to the woman determined to surprise him at every turn.

"Stay behind me. Use my body as a shield." He locked his gaze on those beautiful hazel eyes before Jane could climb out of the SUV. "If you feel threatened in any way, run for the emergency exit next to the garage door and don't look back."

"Okay." Her hair hid one side of her face. His fingers itched to put it back where it belonged. But he wouldn't. No matter how many times he'd thought of touching her, getting mixed up with a client—with *her*—only complicated the situation. He wasn't about to take that chance. For her own safety and his brother's memory, he couldn't do it. "What about you?"

Sullivan cleared his head. *Keep her safe.*

*Eliminate the threat. Nothing more.* "Don't worry about me. I can take care of myself."

"As you clearly showed on the way to your cabin." A smile brightened her features.

"I knew you were going to throw that almost dying thing back in my face," he said.

Her smile disappeared. She shot her hand out to rest on his arm before he could climb from the SUV. Sullivan sat paralyzed, hypnotized, as an uncontrollable rush of desire raced up his arm. Despite their past, he was beginning to like it when she touched him. Too much. "Promise me something before we get out of the car."

One hand on the door handle, the other on his weapon, Sullivan narrowed his eyes. "Anything."

He meant it, but he swallowed hard. What was coming his way?

"As a lawyer, I took an oath to uphold the law. Promise me we're going to bring this guy to justice." Determination unlike Sullivan had ever seen sharpened her jawline, and a chill swept down his spine. "Legally."

"That is the one thing I can't promise, Jane." He stepped out onto the pavement. He controlled *his* actions. God-given agency prevented him from doing that for someone else.

So whether or not Christopher Menas saw the inside of a jail cell rather than the inside of a coffin was up to him. Not Sullivan.

He took point, with Jane close on his heels and Anthony taking up the rear. They moved as one toward the elevator doors, the only way into the main building from the garage. Blackhawk Security was one of the most protected buildings in the world. Then again, Jane had walked right into his office last night without setting off the alarms.

Which begged the question, how had a JAG Corps prosecutor gotten past his security? And how had she uncovered his true identity to blackmail him in the first place?

SOMETIMES MEMORIES WERE the worst form of torture.

Jane dropped her head against her palm and brought her knees into her chest while she sat on the couch outside Blackhawk Security's main conference room. Sullivan's team had been holed up in there for two hours now. Coming up with a plan. She had wanted to be part of the meeting, but Sullivan wouldn't budge— Blackhawk agents only.

She closed her eyes against the flashes of all

those photos on Christopher Menas's wall, photos he'd taken of *her*.

Her stomach rolled. Exhaustion tore at her from the inside, her clothes smelled of smoke and she hadn't eaten in over twenty-four hours. How much more before the nightmare ended? She wanted her life back.

Raised voices—male voices—penetrated through the glass doors. Jane studied movements between the closed blinds just as the door to the conference room swung open. She straightened.

A thin woman with long blond hair and stiletto heels threw her a sad smile as she sauntered down the hallway in her pencil skirt. She carried files with her, but hollowness in the woman's cheeks and the dark circles under her eyes kept Jane from asking if the files pertained to her case. Grief, thick and strong, clung to the woman, and Jane wouldn't stop her in the middle of her escape.

A handful of Sullivan's team trickled past the door frame and down the hall. She'd met Anthony, the tall, silent statue of muscle who wouldn't spare her a glimpse from behind those dark sunglasses of his, but the others weren't familiar. Another woman, this one with shoulder-length brown hair and a strong jawline, kept her head down in her own files as she followed the blonde. Had to be Elizabeth, the NSA analyst Sullivan had called to trace the call to Jane's cell phone. The lone man left behind—muscular, handsome with wild brown hair and tan skin—headed straight toward her.

Sullivan trailed the group out of the conference room, staring at her as she stood. "Jane, this is Vincent Kalani, our forensics expert."

"Nice to finally meet you." His Hawaiian accent surrounded her in a trusting vice as Vincent offered his hand. The peacoat he kept drawn up around his neck attempted to cover the dark tattoos flowing artistically down his neck but failed. Deep lines creased his forehead as he studied her from head to toe. Not sexually, but almost as though he'd been waiting for this moment between them for a long time. "I feel like I know you already."

"Oh?" Jane took his hand. Rough. Worn around the edges. Just like his dark brown eyes. Dropping his grip, she crossed her arms over her midsection. Something about Sullivan's forensics expert raised her defenses. Like he really did know her...and all of her secrets.

"Vincent is the one I sent to your town house to collect evidence your stalker had left behind after breaking in. He worked for the NYPD, so he's familiar with cases like yours." Sullivan maneuvered to her side, his hand planting on her lower back, and she couldn't help the tiny flood of comfort from his touch. "Tell her what you found."

"Aside from the fact you hide massive amounts of chocolate-chip cookie dough in a drawer at the back of your fridge," Vincent said, straight-faced, "nothing."

"What?" Jane uncrossed her arms. Pressure built behind her sternum the longer the forensics expert refused to elaborate. "What do you mean 'nothing'? He was in my house. I have the proof on my phone—"

"Everything in your home has been wiped clean." Handing her a manila file folder, he nodded toward it. "No fingerprints. No hairs. Nothing in your carpets left from shoes. No fibers left around." Vincent shifted his weight as she read the file, lowering his voice. "Not even yours."

"That's not possible." She snapped her head up. Checking the address at the top of Vincent's report, she closed the file. Her gut instincts kicked into overdrive. She didn't have to read the rest of the report to figure out where this was going. It was written all over the forensics expert's face, in the way he'd held her hand a little too tightly a few moments ago, in the way he studied her now, looking for a crack in her expression. She was a lawyer. She'd attended her fair share of interrogations over the years. Pointing the report toward Vincent, she leveled her gaze with his. "You think I'm hiding something."

Not a question. She'd heard part of an argument from outside the conference room while the Blackhawk Security team deliberated what to do about her next. Her grip tightened on the folder, and she slid her attention to Sullivan. Did he trust her? Or Vincent? "And you? I assume you read the report. After everything we've been through the past day and a half, the accident, the fire, what do you think?"

"I can't forget you kept Christopher Menas's name from us." Arms crossed over his chest, stance wide, Sullivan's expression turned defensive. He exhaled hard, but refused to look at her, attention on Vincent's report. "I have to look at every possibility and, as of right now, we don't have the evidence to confirm Christopher Menas is after you. Both the tow truck and the photos could've been used to frame him." His eyes shifted to Vincent. "This could be someone's way to get back at Menas for skipping his sentencing and not paying for what he did ten years ago."

Not someone. Her. An invisible knife twisted in her stomach. Jane held her ground, but she wasn't sure how much longer she could stand there. She rolled her fingers into the center of her palm to keep the betrayal working up her throat at bay. "I see. So I hired someone to T-bone us in that intersection, putting my life at risk, took all those photos of myself and hung them in his apartment, then set the fire while you and Elliot weren't looking?"

"You're a smart woman, Ms. Reise," Vincent said. "Top of your class at University of Washington School of Law, instant promotion during your enlistment. It's not difficult to imagine a scenario where you might want revenge on a man who ran from his crimes." He took a single step toward her, most likely trying to intimidate her with his six-foot-plus frame, but it wouldn't work. She was the Full Metal Bitch. Her gaze flickered to Sullivan, and Jane's insides froze. It wouldn't work. "Is that why you came to Blackhawk Security?"

"It's *Captain* Reise." Jane notched her chin higher, her voice more confident than she felt inside. "And I have no idea what you're talking about. I already told Sullivan why I came to him. He has the skills to catch whoever is doing this to me."

"See, now, I think it's more than that." Vincent shoved his hands into his coat. "As Sullivan has just informed us, you were the lead prosecutor on Marrok Warren's case. You hated the fact Sullivan blamed you for his brother's death, and now you're here to make it look like you're the victim. Or is it a coincidence you moved to Anchorage shortly after Sullivan was discharged from the navy?"

Her jaw wobbled, but Jane clamped it tight. This wasn't about Marrok. This wasn't about her and Sullivan. This was about survival. Turning to Sullivan, Jane pushed every ounce of strength she had left into her voice and stared straight into those sea-blue-colored eyes, the eyes she'd started to trust. Foolishly.

"If blaming victims is how you insist on running your security firm, then I made a mistake in relying on you for help." Jane headed for the elevators down the hall, but stopped alongside a fake ficus tree and turned her attention over her shoulder. "Run my phone records, check my email or get my financials. Do whatever you have to do. Do it and then call me when you figure out who's trying to kill me."

Sullivan's eyes widened a split second before she turned, forcing her feet to slow as she headed toward the elevators. He followed after her. "Where are you going?"

"I'm not standing around here waiting for whoever is after me to find me again. I haven't slept or eaten in over a day." She punched the button for the elevator to take her to the main floor but refused to look back at him. Instead, she watched the red LED lights shift into different numbers and focused on keeping her eyes dry. "I'm going home. Don't follow me."

# Chapter Six

Jane wasn't responsible for any of this.

He'd known the second she'd given his team permission to run phone records and financials, and to sift through her laptop. Vincent had pushed too hard, but questioning her motives had been the only way to clear Jane's name from the suspect list. There'd been too many coincidences so far in this case and too many ways it'd gone south. How had Menas known to wait for them at that light? How had he found them at the cabin? And how the hell had he gotten the upper hand on them at the apartment?

A short growl resonated deep in his chest as Sullivan pounded his fist into the door three times, his face square in the peephole's focus. Interrogating Jane had been the last thing on his mind when he'd stepped into that conference room, and he'd made that perfectly clear to his team. But the evidence—or lack thereof—spoke volumes. They were dealing with a professional.

The door ripped open. And time froze. Damn, she was a sight for sore eyes.

"I thought I told you not to follow me." Jane leaned against the door, showing off her lean, athletic shape and a hint of skin from under her T-shirt, which she realized and straightened.

"Can I come in?" His insides vibrated with the need to touch her, to ensure he hadn't broken the trust they'd forged over the last couple days, however ridiculous that sounded.

"Let me guess." She crossed her arms over her chest, accentuating the fact she wasn't wearing a bra, but didn't move to let him past the door. "You're here to tell me you uncovered something else that points to me framing Christopher Menas so I can have my own sick revenge."

"I'm sorry about before." And Sullivan meant it. "You've officially been taken off our suspect list. It won't happen again."

Nodding once, Jane moved aside to let him in.

Mentally punching himself in the face, he pushed past her and scanned the town house for signs of forced entry. A window, the back

French doors, anything. But Jane had everything locked up tight. The three-bedroom, two-and-a-half-bathroom rental reflected a vibrant personality. Lots of color, fake flowers, geometric-style pillows. Nothing like the bare walls of his cabin or the emptiness of his office. The thick scent of vanilla surrounded him. The entire house smelled of it. Of her. He spun back toward her, determined to say what he'd come to say and get out before he didn't have the mind to leave. "If it makes you feel any better, I had Elizabeth scour your records, and everything checks out."

A loud beep filled the living room. She brushed against his arm on her way toward the kitchen and opened the microwave. "Someone has tried to kill me two times in the last two days. Nothing short of my stash of cookie dough will make me feel better, if Vincent didn't steal it."

Slamming the microwave door closed, she stuck a fork into whatever she'd nuked and blew on it to cool it down, which shouldn't seem so damn sexy, but right here, right now, Jane was home. She looked relaxed in her sweatpants and T-shirt, hair slightly wet. He'd obviously caught her coming out of the shower. Too bad his own self-hatred had kept him parked outside her house until a few minutes ago. He could've—

"How is Elliot doing?" she asked.

"He'll pull through. He's too stubborn to let a little blow to the head get the best of him, but that's not why I'm here." Resting his hands on his hips, Sullivan focused on her eyes instead of the way her sweatpants hung off her hips. "I need to know how you broke into my office two days ago and where you got your intel on my real name."

Her gaze snapped to his—alarmed—but she covered her surprise faster than he thought possible for a woman who chased the truth for a living. "Because you still think I'm bent on revenge or you're genuinely curious?"

"I've installed a top-of-the-line security system, rigged hundreds of cameras and have around-the-clock security on every floor in that building." Sullivan slowly closed the space between them. His heart rate sped up as though he'd just run a marathon, and he couldn't slow it down. She held her ground but tilted her head back to stare straight up at him without giving anything away. Her sweet scent washed over him, and Sullivan couldn't help but lean into her further. He'd been shot at, tortured, endured physical nightmares and watched men on his team die right in front of him. All without his pulse raising a single beat. How was it possible Jane affected him like this? "There's no way you could've gotten past that system without triggering one of my alarms. Not to mention I buried the files on my old life and my family so deep, not even the CIA could get their hands on them."

"You're right. You have the best security in the world. It's impossible. But the files? That didn't take very much digging at all." Those hazel eyes stayed glued to him, her voice rich and gravelly with exhaustion. A playful sweep of her fingertips across his shoulder froze the air in his lungs. "But I'm not about to give away all my secrets until I can trust you."

Sullivan straightened his spine. "You seem awfully confident for a woman who was accused of orchestrating her own stalking a few hours ago."

"If you believed Vincent's report that I set this whole thing up, that I moved here to change your mind about me—" the playfulness disappeared from Jane's expression "—then you wouldn't have stood up for me against your team in that conference room."

He couldn't argue with that. The instincts that'd been beaten into him during his enlistment in the navy screamed her innocence. She didn't have anything to do with Christopher Menas or whoever was behind this trying to make her life a living hell. She was the victim here.

"Now, if you're hungry, I have more microwavable mush in the freezer. Unless you're into peanut-butter-and-jelly sandwiches." Putting some distance between them, Jane held up a thin black tray with what looked like chicken nuggets, mashed potatoes and a warm brownie. "That is, if you don't want to go back to sitting in your SUV all night, eating beef jerky."

"You saw me?" Tingling spread across his chest. Another smile pulled at the corners of his mouth as Sullivan drove his hands into his jacket pockets. Of course she'd seen him. This wasn't just any client he was dealing with. This was a woman who'd received death threats every day of her career. That brand of work required her to keep her instincts on alert and a gun under her pillow. *His* kind of woman. "And here I thought I had good surveillance skills."

"I've been stalked across the world by a crazed psychopath for the past three months. I'm bound to notice one of your SUVs parked for a couple hours two blocks down the street. Besides, I'm not stupid. I wouldn't have come home and let my guard down long enough to shower if I hadn't known there'd be backup." Jane shoved a forkful of dessert into her mouth, eyes bright, her delectable mouth curling into a smile. "Would you judge me if I said I only bought these meals for the brownie?"

Sullivan straightened. "Across the world?"

Her smile didn't last long. "Guess I left that part out, didn't I?" Lowering her fork back to the plastic dish, she wiped her fingers across her mouth. "Vincent wasn't totally wrong about my moving to Anchorage." Alarm flooded her features. "I mean, I didn't move here in some sick attempt to get you to forgive me for what happened to Marrok. I came here because I started noticing things missing from my quarters back in Afghanistan. At first, it was little things. One of my hair ties, some pieces of clothing." She set her food on the edge of the small round kitchen table a few feet away and crossed her arms under her breasts. "Then my service weapon was stolen. A .40 Smith & Wesson. I asked to be put on leave for personal reasons and came to find you. And to blackmail you if you wouldn't help."

"Your stalker tracked you down in Afghanistan, then followed you to the States?" Sullivan made a mental note to check Menas's travel records, phone records, credit cards, anything that could put him in the Middle East the same time as Jane. Would've been good information to know from the start, but they hadn't exactly gotten the chance to dive deeper into Menas's life before it'd literally gone up in flames.

"I can't think of anyone who would hate me this much. Aside from you." Jane crossed her arms over her chest once again, the strength in her forearms apparent. The apprehension clouding those beautiful eyes singed him right down to the core. "Hey, maybe you're the one stalking me."

"I tried hating you." Sullivan noted the flash of sadness across her features and locked his jaw tight. "Didn't stick after you saved my life back at the cabin. Then ran into a wall of flames to save my private investigator."

Her features brightened as she picked up her forgotten dinner. "Then since you're not here to turn me into the police and I'm not telling you how I broke into your office or uncovered your real name, why are you still here, Sullivan?"

"You're not safe here. This guy knows you. He knows things he shouldn't—"

"Doesn't seem like I'm safe anywhere right now. At your cabin, on the move. I might as well find a small bit of comfort in my own house as long as I can." Yellow lighting reflected off the line of water welling in her lower lash line. Her shoulders sagged as she tossed her meal back onto the table. "It doesn't matter where I go. Whoever wants me dead is going to find me."

"Not if I have anything to do with it." The darkness in her beauty compelled him to close the small amount of space between them and he stepped into her. Sullivan framed her sharp features with calloused hands, those troubled eyes of hers widening. His blood pumped hard through his veins as he breathed her in. His last memory of his brother pulsed at the back of his mind. But right then, all he could think about was chasing the shadows from Jane's gaze. Stupid really.

"We should get some sleep." Jane pulled back, mere centimeters between them, breathing heavy. "You're welcome to take the couch and anything in the fridge."

He clamped his grip around her arms, not willing to let her leave yet. She was soft but strong, the kind of woman who could hold her own in a fight. "Even the cookie dough?"

"Sure. I guess you deserve it." Her lips curled into a smile. "But I'm still not telling you how I broke into your office."

Sullivan used every ounce of control left in

his body to take a step back. Damn, he was a sucker for pain. Getting involved with a client—with Jane at all—was possibly the worst idea he'd ever had. But the sight of her when she'd opened the door had unleashed everything he'd tried to bury since he'd pulled his gun on her two nights ago. Desire. Hope. Life. "Give me a clue?"

"All right. I'll give you one clue, but that's all you get." She hooked her hands behind his neck and pulled herself into him. Shifting her weight to her toes, Jane raised her mouth to his ear, her exhale tickling his already sensitized skin. "It wasn't as hard as you might think."

JANE ENTERED HER bedroom with slow, determined steps and shut the door behind her. But no amount of space from Sullivan eased her racing heart. Had she really imagined kissing him?

She leaned against the door and thunked her head a little harder than she intended. Pain radiated across the back of her head and down her neck, but still didn't dislodge the rampant desire flooding her veins. Offering Sullivan her couch for the night probably wasn't the best idea. It'd been at least ten minutes since he'd taken her face in his hands, but the heat in her lower abdomen still hadn't cooled.

But she couldn't go down that path. Her life depended on her keeping her emotional distance. She exhaled his clean scent from her system and immediately felt better. Swiping the hair out of her face, Jane wrenched the bifold door of her closet back and punched in the six-digit code to her firearm safe. She'd meant every word when she'd told Sullivan that her stalker would find her.

Because she intended to let him.

It'd been the reason she returned home. Whoever was doing this to her had already shown a willingness to harm bystanders. She only hoped Sullivan had the resources and the manpower to protect her neighbors and to get the job done since she'd vastly underestimated the man coming after her. They both had. But not anymore.

No place was more comfortable and familiar to her than her own home. Yes, her stalker had broken in. Had probably searched the place. But she was the one who lived there and knew every detail of her town house.

It was much better than trying to lay a trap somewhere new.

Wrapping her fingers around the .40 Smith & Wesson—similar to the one her stalker had stolen in Afghanistan—she dropped the magazine out, then slammed it back into place. The drill had been burned into her muscle memory for years. She could strip down and reassemble any weapon in the US military arsenal, but her own personal firearm would have to do for tonight. The steel warmed in her hand. It'd been a long time since she'd had to shoot first and ask questions later, but tonight was about survival.

Not the fact that Sullivan Bishop was downstairs on her couch.

"Keep it together a little while longer, Reise." Jane placed the gun under her pillow, brushed her teeth and climbed into bed. The cold sheets raised goose bumps along her arms. Nothing like Sullivan's hot, hair-raising touch. Her mind raced with different ways she could make that particular fantasy come true. All she had to do was go down to her living room.

Nope. Not going there. Tossing onto her side, Jane stared into the lens of the small camera she'd installed a few minutes before Sullivan pounded on her front door. Her stalker had already broken in once. Wouldn't happen again. Stay awake. Finish this once and for all. Get on with her life. And Sullivan...

She shoved her nose into her T-shirt and inhaled deep, clinging to the remnants of his scent on her clothing. They could cross that road when there wasn't blackmail and a life-threatening stalker hanging over their heads.

Visions of his magnetic blue eyes danced across the back of her eyelids. Exhaustion pulled at her, her body aching for sweet relief. It'd been more than twenty-four hours since she'd had the chance to lie down, but she couldn't give in to sleep yet. The camera would catch her stalker on video—give them concrete evidence Christopher Menas was behind this—but the gun under her pillow would put an end to this sick game.

DEAFENING SILENCE WOKE HER.

Jane rubbed her eyes with the heels of her hands. Crap, she'd fallen asleep. Reaching for the S&W tucked under her pillow, she sat up straight. Fog clouded her brain, but not so much as to not realize what was missing. Where was her gun? She spun for the lamp on the nightstand and twisted the knob, checking the rest of the bed.

A crisp white piece of paper lay beside an all-too-familiar .40 S&W handgun on the pillow. She'd recognize that gun anywhere. Her stolen service weapon.

Her heart hiccuped.

Five words in block letters. "You're going to need this."

He'd been here. In her house. Maybe even touched her.

She couldn't breathe. Couldn't think. Covering her mouth with the back of her arm, Jane fought the bile climbing up her throat. This was what she'd wanted, why she'd come home, but the reality gutted her from the inside. How had her stalker gotten past Sullivan? Snapping her attention toward the cracked bedroom door, Jane wrapped her hand around the gun and threw off the sheets. "Sullivan."

If something had happened to him, she'd never forgive herself for dragging him into this mess.

The soft echo of the front door closing propelled her out of bed. The intruder was still close by. Grip tight on the gun, Jane ripped out of her room and ran after the shadow disappearing through the front door. He wouldn't slip away this time.

Freezing November air slammed against her, but she pumped her legs hard without missing a beat. No more games. No more fear. Gravel cut into her bare feet as she chased after the figure up ahead. He passed under a streetlamp, heading south. Thick black jacket, Huskies ball cap, short brown hair. She was too far away to get much else and ground her back molars as she pushed herself harder. Her stalker ducked into a short alley between two single-family houses, but he wouldn't lose her that easily. "Christopher!"

The breath that heaved in and out of her lungs crystallized into large, white puffs in front of her mouth as she slowed. Her skin tingled with the sudden change in temperature, but Jane wasn't going back to her town house. Not yet. She pressed herself into the wall outside the alleyway. She'd memorized this neighborhood and every escape route the day she'd moved in. Her stalker obviously hadn't taken the same precautions. The alley ended at the back of a Chinese restaurant with no other access unless he broke into the large factory directly north of there. There was nowhere for him to run.

Jane angled her head around the corner, but moonlight and streetlamps cut off at the top of the houses. She couldn't see anything. Surveying the rest of the street, she took a deep breath. Hints of spicy aftershave hung on the air, pulling at memories of first love, suspicions, then terror. She remembered that aftershave from college, from Christopher's skin. But why come after her now? It didn't make sense.

With another look down the alley, her instincts screamed for her to go back home. No sign of the man who'd run from her. Something wasn't right, like Christopher had lured her to this point for a reason. But why?

"Jane!" Sullivan pounded up the street toward her.

The tension running down her spine lessened. He'd chew her out for running after a crazed stalker on her own, but a small part of her was relieved he'd followed her. And he wasn't hurt.

Lowering her weapon, Jane relaxed in defeat and sunk her weight against the house. She glanced one last time into the alley. Christopher was still just playing games with her. Trying to keep her scared, confused. Vulnerable. And it'd worked. He'd lured her out of the house. She shook her head as though she could rewind the past few minutes. She'd let emotion get in the way of catching the man responsible for turning her world upside down. How could she have been so stupid? Shoving off from the wall, she stepped toward the road to head Sullivan off. "Over here—"

"Hello, Janey." A hand clamped around her mouth, then another around her waist, pulling her against a wall of muscle.

Jane struggled against her attacker's grip as he dragged her into the depths of the alleyway, darkness closing around her.

# Chapter Seven

Sullivan was either going to kill Jane for running out the door with a loaded gun by herself or kiss her. He'd decide when he found her. He stumbled out the front door, gun in hand, but the world tilted on its axis. He hit the ground hard. Whatever drug he'd been injected with still hadn't cleared his system. The intruder had come through the front door. No forced entry—like they'd had a key. Every second played in his mind on slow repeat. Sullivan had shot up from the couch, clicked off the safety on his weapon and took a single step forward. But whoever had broken in had been two steps ahead of him. The syringe had emptied into his neck before he'd even had a chance to counter. He'd crumpled right there on the floor. Paralyzed but alert. His mind had gone to a dark place while he'd watched Jane run out the door and he lay there. Useless.

What the hell had he been shot up with? A mild paralyzer?

Menas had come into Jane's home, had terrorized her for the last three months. The bastard was going to find out exactly what kind of monster Sullivan had kept locked up the past decade.

Adrenaline pumped hard through his veins as he burst through the foot of snow in Jane's front yard, only the sound of his breathing loud in his ears. A cramp shot up his right calf muscle, curling his toes inside his boots, but he pushed through. Pain, exhaustion and stiffness clawed at him from the inside, his vision blurry, but he wouldn't stop until he found Jane alive.

There were no other options.

Shuffling down one of the alleys to his left claimed his attention. The man behind these mind games wasn't an idiot. He'd known Sullivan would be there to protect his target and had drugged him to keep him out of the fight. Wasn't happening. Sullivan fanned his grip around the gun, index finger planted beside the trigger. Anticipation vibrated down his spine. This was what he did best, what he enjoyed doing. For his country. For his clients. For Jane.

What was it about her that he couldn't seem to hate? After everything she put him through—

was *still* putting him through—she deserved it. But he couldn't hate her. Not such a strong, intelligent, vulnerable woman. She needed his help. She needed *him*. And nothing would stop him from getting to her.

Back pressed to one of the houses, Sullivan checked the alleyway. No sign of movement, but that didn't mean anything. Her stalker might've knocked Jane unconscious or— No. Sullivan wouldn't go there. Shoulders pulled back, gun up, he kept low and moved fast. His right foot dragged behind slightly, the last of the paralysis taking its sweet time leaving his system. Would've been easy to finish the job back at the town house with Sullivan unable to fight back, but apparently Jane's stalker didn't want him dead. Which he fully intended to take advantage of.

But where was Jane? Sullivan held his weapon steady, closing in on the alleyway one slow step at a time. "I'll give you three seconds to show your face before I start shooting. There's nowhere left to run. We know who you are and why you're doing this. And I'll hunt you down as long as it takes to put you behind bars."

Another round of shuffling said he was in the right place, and he swung the gun to his right. Pain shot up his neck and spidered throughout the base of his skull. He fought to stay upright and keep his weapon level.

But a wall of flesh slammed into him.

He hit the side of the building, the air knocked from his lungs. The gun slid across the pavement as blow after blow rained down on him from the shadow armed with a metal pipe. Sullivan held his forearm out to block the hits. Heart thundering in his ears, he swept one leg out and unbalanced his attacker.

The man went down, landing on his left arm. The crack of bone filled the few short seconds of silence just before deep groans reverberated off the walls, but it didn't keep his attacker down for long. A glint of metal flashed. The man had traded his pipe for a knife.

Sullivan pushed to his feet, pulling out his own knife, which he kept strapped to his ankle, and flipped the blade outward. He swung it parallel to his wrist and moved in, legs spread, torso angled to make himself a smaller target. His attacker did the same, and Sullivan hesitated.

Christopher Menas didn't have military training according to his records, yet this man almost mirrored Sullivan in his movements. The first swipe came fast, but Sullivan blocked it and shoved his attacker's arm down, striking out with a fist to the man's face. Shadows played across his attacker's black ski mask as Sullivan countered, slicing the blade across the man's chest.

Another groan filled the alleyway, but the injury didn't slow his opponent. He charged at full speed.

Sullivan kicked out, slamming his boot into the man's kneecap to keep from getting tackled. He barely registered the remnants of the drug in his system, but another swipe from his attacker's blade landed home. Stinging pain lanced through his biceps, but disappeared as his body's fight-or-flight response surged through his blood again.

No more games. Jane could be anywhere by now. Could be hurt.

He lunged forward, shoulders low, and hiked his attacker over his shoulder and into the alleyway wall. Hard. An elbow slammed into his spine. Two times. Three. Sullivan's knees buckled, and he forced all of his momentum into rolling his attacker over his head. With one foot planted in the man's stomach, he tossed the masked assailant as far as he could, using his attacker's momentum to roll himself on top.

Only his attacker had the same idea.

Sullivan's vision blurred as he spun, landing pinned under his opponent against the cold, wet asphalt. In the span of half a breath, his attacker plunged the blade down toward Sullivan's sternum, but Sullivan caught his wrist a split second before the knife hit home. His muscles burned as he held the blade above his chest. Sullivan was stronger, but whoever was on top of him leveraged everything he had into putting that blade into his chest. Sweat dripped into his eyes, the air in his lungs frozen.

He wouldn't lose this battle. Not when Jane's life depended on him. Sullivan hiked his right knee into his attacker's rib cage, dislodging the man's hold on him. He slipped out from under the knife and shot to his feet. He wrapped his hand around his opponent's neck, flipped him over and planted his knee into the man's spine. Moonlight glinted off his blade as he placed it at his attacker's throat.

Convulsed breaths echoed throughout the alleyway.

"Where is she? Where is Jane?" The words left his mouth as a growl. The urge to tear, to rip—to protect what was his—surged through his blood. And the man pinned beneath him looked a lot like prey. Sullivan clenched the man's ski mask and ripped it over his head. Pulling his attacker into the circle of light from the streetlamp, he swayed on his feet. He breathed through his nose, slowing down his heart rate to keep his head on straight. His fingers went numb for a moment as he studied the man in his grasp. A hard exhale rushed from him, but he tightened his grip on his attacker. "You're not Christopher Menas. Who the hell are you?"

Bubbling laughter filled the alleyway. An older, darker face, nowhere close to Menas's thirty-four years of age, contorted in pain as the man in his grip fought to look up at Sullivan, a crooked smile spreading across his face. "I don't kill and tell."

"A contract killer. Great." He should've known. No way Menas would've been able to defend himself like that. Jane's stalker was a tow truck operator. No military experience. But none of this made sense. How did Menas even get in contact with a mercenary? Shoving the blade under the man's throat, Sullivan leaned in close. "Where is Jane?"

A sniper's laser sight slipped over the mercenary's shoulder, and Sullivan reacted by instinct. He dropped the knife and swung the man in his grip around. Two bullets ripped through his attacker's back, the shots rocking Sullivan with two strong thumps.

A glint of moonlight reflected back toward him from the roof of the warehouse across the street, but disappeared a split second later. Another slow exhale worked to bring his heart rate under control. A scope. Had to be another contracted mercenary cleaning up the loose ends. But where did that leave Jane?

Sullivan discarded the man he'd used as a human shield and stepped over the body. Sweeping his weapon into his hand, he stalked toward the factory at the north end of the alleyway. With a single tap on the device lodged in his ear, he had his weapons expert on the other line. "We've got new players. One of them just took a shot at me. Warehouse north of Jane's town house. Bring the shooter to me."

"Done." Anthony hung up. No time to waste.

Loud pops cracked in Sullivan's neck as he wrenched his head from side to side. Didn't matter how many mercenaries Menas had hired to protect himself. The bastard could have an entire army behind him for all Sullivan cared. It wouldn't stop him from getting to Jane.

JANE THREW HER elbow back with as much force as she could but hit solid muscle and Kevlar. Digging her fingernails into her attacker's wrist, she swung her legs wide and threw her weight forward in an attempt to unbalance him. Didn't work. The man squeezing the air from her chest was so much bigger and so much stronger than she was. No amount of escape attempts seemed to faze him as he pulled her across the wide expanse of the factory.

"Did you think you could get away from me that easily? I'm not the man you claimed you loved back in college anymore, Jane. I've changed. Traveled. Killed people. Made some new friends." The eerily familiar voice closed in on her right ear and sent a shiver down her spine. Christopher Menas. "Besides, I've been waiting too long for this chance."

"Christopher, please. It doesn't have to be like this." Her bare heels caught on chunks of broken cement as she struggled to loosen his forearm grip around her collarbone. The sour scent of cigarettes dived deep into her lungs with every panicked inhale. He'd already dragged her halfway through the sheet metal factory, weaving between large pieces of machinery she'd never seen before. Any deeper and Sullivan wouldn't be able to track her. Because he was coming for her. She had to believe that. Stall. Get Christopher to slow down. Give Sullivan a chance.

"Sure it does, Janey." Her insides flipped at the nickname he'd used for her all throughout their relationship, but not in the way it used to. He didn't sound the same, didn't feel the same as she remembered. Christopher pulled up short and swung her around to face him.

His dark brown eyes flashed as a stream of molten metal poured into a base a few feet away. It was late. Usually only a few factory workers kept an eye on operations overnight, but the unhinged mania in Christopher's gaze said it all. He'd kill anyone who got in his way. She couldn't risk dragging innocent lives into this. Sweat glistened down his stern features as he stared at her. He was right. He wasn't the same man she'd given her heart to all those years ago. Familiar angles and planes of his face were still there, but he'd filled out. A lot. The Kevlar vest he'd strapped on struggled to rein in the muscle underneath and intensified the in-depth story of tattoos covering every inch of his now-massive arms. Scars interrupted the thick five-o'clock shadow across his jaw, as well as his eyebrows, and his hair had receded several inches. The man staring her down with hell in his gaze was dangerous. Perhaps psychotic. Definitely not the tow truck operator she'd had in mind when she and Sullivan had pinned him as her stalker less than twelve hours ago. "And don't worry about your bodyguard. My friends certainly know how to show a guy like him a good time."

Friends? Her heart sank. *Sullivan.*

"What did you do?" She ripped out of his grasp and, surprisingly, Christopher let her go. No point in running. He'd wound them through a maze of machinery she had no idea how to escape. Probably for that reason alone. He'd catch her without trying, and she'd have wasted precious time in getting to Sullivan.

At least four knives and just as many handguns peeked out from under his jacket and from the pockets of his cargo pants. What had her ex turned himself into? A mercenary? Flipping his wrist over, he read his watch. Christopher reached for her again and hauled her into his chest. Her sternum hit his Kevlar with a thud. "We've got such plans for you."

*We?*

"Are you going to kill me?" *Keep him talking. Keep him distracted.* Jane snaked her hand around to his closest pocket. Loud hissing sounds from the nearest machine drew Christopher's attention to his left and he reached for one of the many sidearms haphazardly packed into his gear. Not in control. Too easy to scare. Dangerous. Her fingertips scraped over the butt of a large blade in his pants, but Jane couldn't wrap her hand around the grip without tipping Christopher off. Her throat tightened, his cigarette breath fanning across her cheek.

"Not yet." He slid back from her. Jane let his own movements draw the knife into her hand. "First—" wrapping his bruising strength around her arm again, he shoved her ahead of him "—we've got a chopper to catch."

"I'm not going anywhere with you." Jane swung fast, arcing the blade straight across Christopher's face. He doubled over to the side as she hit her target, his scream nearly bursting her eardrums. Fleeing, Jane pumped her legs hard, exhaustion from the insufferable heat around her already pulling at her muscles. Grip tight around the knife, she mentally ticked off the different machines Christopher had dragged her past on the way in. There had to be a way out of this maze.

The factory's windows had been blacked out. No sign of an exit. No idea which way they'd come in. She couldn't just run from a crazed maniac until she lucked out with an exit. She needed a plan. The aggressive hissing and movements of the machines covered any sounds Christopher might've made from following her. Jane checked over her shoulder. She couldn't see him but ducked behind one of the larger machines for cover. Air dragged through her windpipe as her heart fought to keep up with the rest of her body. She'd kept in shape over the years, but running on pure adrenaline would only take her so far.

Okay, luring Christopher to her town house hadn't been the best idea. But then again, she hadn't expected him to be a mercenary either. None of Sullivan's or his team's research into her ex had hinted as much. Although, now that she thought about it, there was a piece of her that always believed she'd see his name on the FBI's Most Wanted List someday.

"Janey…" he said, taunting. Her name on his lips pooled dread in her stomach. "That wasn't very nice." He sounded close all of a sudden— too close.

Her spine straightened, and she pressed her back into the machine behind her. Heat seared her skin, but Jane clamped her mouth shut. She couldn't call out, couldn't give away her position. If she had to guess, she'd ended up at the south end of the building. She studied the blade in her hand, the edge tinted red. There wasn't an exit on the south end. At least, not one she'd noted mapping out her neighborhood when she'd first moved in.

Where was Sullivan? She had no doubt the

former SEAL could take care of himself, but neither of them had calculated the addition of Christopher's "friends."

Footsteps echoed nearby, and her surroundings came into a sharp focus. She breathed deeply, evenly, as a deadly calm descended over the factory floor. Sweat dripped from her eyebrows. The blade's handle grew slick in her hand. She needed to get to the exit, needed to find Sullivan.

"Janey." A shadow passed in front of her faster than she thought possible. Christopher knocked the knife from her hand and clamped his grip around her throat. Shoving her hard against the machine at her back, he let the skin across her shoulder blades sizzle from the blistering heat for a few seconds. Searing pain lightninged throughout her upper body, but Jane couldn't scream with her air supply cut off.

She fought for breath, vision blurry, but this close, she realized she'd slashed a deep cut into his right cheekbone. And the look in his near-black eyes along with the hand still around her throat said he intended to make her pay. But the second she gave in would be the end of her. She wasn't getting on whatever chopper he had waiting for her. No matter what. Mentally checking off all the ways to counter an attack, Jane unclamped her hands from around his wrist and went for his eyes. She dug the fingernails of her thumbs into his eye sockets, then kneed him in the groin.

Christopher's grip lightened but didn't let go as another scream ripped up his throat. And before she knew what was coming, his other hand slammed into her jawline. "You shouldn't have done that. I promised to bring you in alive. Not untouched."

She hit the heated cement floor—hard—sparks and hot metal brightening up the dark edges of her vision. His rough exhales drowned out the overwhelming pounding in her head. A single kick to her rib cage pushed the air from her lungs and shut down any other ideas of her fighting back. Jane rolled into the fetal position to prevent another hit, but the damage had already been done. Pain unlike anything she'd experienced washed over her, her vision going white for a few seconds. She couldn't breathe. Couldn't think.

"You've got a lot more spunk in you than I remember." Christopher crouched over her, slipping the blade she'd stolen from his pants back to its rightful place. "Where was this girl when we were dating? I might not have had to go after your roommates if you'd shown me a little bit of a challenge."

Her lungs spasmed out of paralysis from the kick to her midsection, gulping down heated air. She couldn't stop fighting, couldn't let him take her. Because, from the deadly look in his expression, the chances of her getting out alive were not in her favor. A single name crossed her mind as tears welled in her eyes. Where was he? Was he alive? "Sullivan…"

"Dead," he said.

*No, no, no, no. Not Sullivan.* "No."

"Yes." Christopher's scarred features closed in on her as he slipped a strand of her hair behind her ear. Her mouth filled with bile at the intimate gesture. The world spun as he wrapped his calloused hands around her arms and hiked her over his shoulder. He straightened, locking her knees against him and her hands in his grasp. "Nobody's coming for you, Janey. You're finally mine."

# Chapter Eight

When Sullivan finally reached the factory, Jane was slumped over a heavily armed man's shoulder. He'd found her.

Tearing across the slick cement factory floor, Sullivan sprinted harder than he had in years. The navy had trained him for any kind of combat, taught him how to successfully shoot his Glock and hit the target from two hundred yards, but risking Jane's life in the process wasn't an option. Unbearable heat dived deep into his lungs, and he inhaled fast to keep oxygen pumping to his extremities. "Jane!"

Thick doors slammed behind the man with Jane in his arms as they disappeared out the west exit. Sullivan pushed himself harder, sweat dripping into his eyes and down his neck. The longer he lost sight of them, the smaller chance he had of recovering her unharmed. He rammed his left shoulder into the steel, slamming the door open into the concrete wall behind him. His heart pounded behind his ears as his lungs devoured the cold, fresh air.

No sign of Jane.

"Jane!" Sullivan ran a hand across his forehead to dispel the sweat now freezing to his skin. No response. Damn it. He couldn't have lost her already. It was impossible. The factory's brightly lit parking lot didn't offer anything in the way of cover. Whoever had Jane couldn't have disappeared with a 120-pound woman that fast on foot. Unless...

Headlights drifted over the right side of his face a split second before a black Audi Q7 barreled straight toward him. Sullivan dived for cover, swinging his gun up and over. He squeezed off four rounds, none of which penetrated the SUV's windows. Bulletproof. The SUV sped across the parking lot, heading for the main road.

He tapped the earpiece connected to the most combat-experienced asset on his team and vaulted after the vehicle on foot. He wouldn't get far on his own, but he wasn't about to give up on Jane either. "Forget the shooter. The package is in a black Audi Q7 heading east toward Seward Highway. License plate is—"

A Blackhawk Security GMC screeched to

a halt in front of him, and Sullivan lunged inside. Anthony Harris, his resident weapons expert, slammed on the accelerator, not waiting for Sullivan to shut the passenger-side door. He twisted the steering wheel, flipping around. "Your shooter is in that vehicle. Hold on to something."

Momentum pinned Sullivan to the back of his seat, and he braced himself against the roof of the SUV as they raced over the speed bumps set throughout the parking lot. Red taillights flashed at least a quarter mile ahead as the Audi spun onto the highway. "Faster, damn it. We can't lose them."

Anthony didn't answer. Always one for taking orders without question. The GMC's engine growled as he pushed it harder, and within seconds they were approaching the highway. They skidded into oncoming traffic, horns and headlights penetrating through the thick cloud of pressure inside the SUV.

"There." Sullivan pointed at the Audi weaving in and out of both lanes of cars. He leaned forward, hoping to catch a glimpse of Jane's outline through the dark tinted windows. No such luck. Majestic snow-covered mountains edged up against the freeway, but it was too dark to see much of anything else. Something wet and sticky tickled the underside of his arm as they maneuvered through traffic. Blood glistened across his skin with the help of the headlights of other cars.

"There's a first-aid kit under your seat," Anthony said, eyes never leaving the road.

Sullivan put pressure on the wound across his arm with his gun hand. "I'm fine. Just find a way to get me closer to the SUV." He would jump on the car's hood if he had to. Although, shooting out the tires should be enough, as long as they weren't armored, as well.

The Audi cut through two lanes of cars. Motorists swerved to avoid hitting others, effectively causing all traffic to skid to a halt. Anthony slammed on the brakes. Bracing himself for impact, Sullivan kept his focus on the SUV now turning onto International Airport Road, one of the only roads leading to Ted Stevens Anchorage International Airport. If her stalker got Jane onto a plane, Sullivan would never see her again. And that wasn't an option. Not today. Not ever.

Screeching tires filled his ears as the GMC skidded at a twenty-degree angle until his weapons expert veered off-road and cut west.

"They're headed for the airport." Sullivan pushed the button to release his seat belt and then climbed into the back seat and unearthed the heavy-duty case of ammunition that traveled anywhere Anthony went. Dropping the magazine out of his Glock, he replaced the expended 9 mm rounds he'd wasted on the bulletproof SUV and slammed the magazine back into place. He flipped open another case that stored three black Kevlar vests and geared up. Two more knives and an extra magazine of rounds fitted into the vest. "I'm not going to even ask if you're armed."

"Don't worry about me," Anthony said. "Get ready. We're going in hard."

Through the windshield, Sullivan watched the distance between the two vehicles shrink fast. Anthony closed in on the Audi's bumper, slamming the back driver's-side quarter panel. The hit rocked through the vehicle, and Sullivan pitched forward between the two front seats. "Hit them again."

The GMC lurched forward and cut off any maneuvering the driver of the Audi had in mind. This was it. No way would that SUV reach the airport. Anthony spun the steering wheel and slammed into the Audi. The SUV fishtailed until the vehicle hit the GMC perpendicular. The tires caught on the pavement and the Audi flipped, two times, three. Air rushed from Sullivan's lungs.

Anthony slammed on the brakes to keep from ramming into the underside of the SUV, but Sullivan was out of the vehicle before the GMC came to a full stop.

Boots heavy on the pavement, he palmed the Glock in his right hand and unsheathed a knife with his left. The sounds of broken glass and heavy breathing consumed his attention, as someone fought to leave the vehicle. Jane was strong, a survivor like him, but the hand clawing its way through the debris wasn't hers. He couldn't think about that right now. Mercs were known to shoot first and ask questions later, and he had to do the same. *Neutralize the threat. Then get to her.*

A car door slammed behind him.

Sullivan clicked off the safety of his gun and aimed without looking back at his weapons expert. The former army Ranger could take care of himself and understood the directive: get the client to safety. At any cost.

The first shots forced Sullivan to take cover behind the GMC's open passenger door. He returned fire, hitting the shooter multiple times. The thick tree line on either side of the road provided deep cover, but Sullivan wasn't about to let any strays escape. The shooting stopped. Nothing but the sound of the wind rustling through the trees reached his ears. This wasn't over. Not by a long shot. He maneuvered around the door, weapon raised, muscles tight.

Two more heavily armed men climbed from the wreckage. Neither had the chance to lift their weapons in defense as Anthony closed in on the vehicle. Seconds passed in silence. Minutes. Where was Jane?

Another round of gunfire spread over the pavement, and Sullivan hit the ground.

"Sullivan!" a familiar voice screamed.

He snapped his head up. "Jane."

Tracking the rushed movements of two shadows as they ran down the road—one with short dark hair—Sullivan pushed up from the asphalt and took off after them. Menas's contract killers had nowhere left to run. The tree line was thinning, the airport was still five miles away, and the woman he held on to only slowed him down. His heart thundered in his ears. Or was that something else?

"Boss!" Anthony called.

A pool of light materialized over Jane and her kidnapper, illuminating the road and the mercenary's identity with blinding light. Christopher Menas. Sullivan clenched his jaw and leaned into the run as the black EC725 Super Cougar helicopter descended over its target—Jane.

Choppers. Mercenaries. Who the hell was this guy?

A spread of bullets flew over his head from behind, but Anthony's attempt to keep the helicopter from landing was in vain. Cougars were built for war, made to repel anything weaker than a Hellfire missile.

If Jane got onto that chopper, he couldn't follow. With a three-hundred-mile range at his fingertips, Menas could take her anywhere in the country, and Sullivan would lose her forever. Not an option.

"Jane!" He swung his arms hard, anything to force his legs to go faster. He was within shooting range to stop Menas but wouldn't risk Jane's life in the process.

She swung her elbow up and back into Menas's face, buying Sullivan a few more seconds, but a backhand to her face knocked her out cold onto the pavement.

A growl worked up Sullivan's throat as he lunged for Menas. He collided with solid muscle and Kevlar but held on to his gun. Straddling the enemy, Sullivan pulled the trigger, but Menas shoved his wrist aside. The bullet hit the asphalt next to Menas's head, and a blow to Sullivan's left side wrenched him off her kidnapper.

Menas straightened, blood running down his cheek from a deep gash. "You must be the great Sullivan Bishop. Heard a lot about you, Frogman."

Sullivan caught the kidnapper's boot as he kicked out and flipped the bastard onto the pavement. Rolling Menas's head between his thighs, he squeezed with as much pressure as he could, taking hit after hit to his kidneys. Outside the pool of light, Anthony collected Jane and ran to the GMC. Mission complete. Time to end this. The pilot of the chopper rushed to help Menas, but Sullivan put one round in each of his legs before the pilot could pull his weapon.

"I have a strict no-abduction policy when it comes to my clients, Menas." Sullivan twisted Menas's arm until a snap sent a shiver down his spine, but, to the bastard's credit, Menas didn't scream. He'd finish this now. For Jane.

A spray of bullets ricocheted off the asphalt at his feet, and Sullivan swung his gun up as he jumped to his feet. He fired three rounds at the second SUV barreling toward the chopper from the other direction. Damn it. Menas must've had another team waiting at the airport. The Glock clicked as he squeezed the trigger.

Empty. He discarded the gun across the road and spun for cover. Tires screeched ahead of him as he took position behind the chopper, return fire whizzing past him to his left. Anthony had him covered, but as two mercenaries exited the SUV and closed in on Menas—raining a nonstop storm of bullets on the GMC—Sullivan recognized the window on ending Jane's nightmare closing fast.

Menas remained motionless in the chopper's spotlight as two members of his team clamped on to his arms and dragged their leader across the pavement toward their escape vehicle, all the while spraying rounds right at Sullivan. He didn't have any other weapons, no way to stop Menas from getting away.

The Blackhawk Security GMC rolled up beside him, Anthony positioned out the driver's-side window to keep the mercs at bay in case they returned fire. Sullivan fought to catch his breath, the aches and pains of fighting overwhelming. Doubling over, he clamped a hand over the gash in his arm, then straightened. Satisfied they were in the clear—for now— his weapons expert leaned across the cab and pushed open the passenger-side door. "Boss, we gotta go. She's not looking good."

Sullivan ignored the open door and slid in beside Jane, attention on the second SUV hauling away from the scene. The brake lights dimmed in the darkness. Menas was gone. Wrapping his arms around her, he checked her pulse and wiped the blood from her skin. Her moan rumbled through him, hiking his heart into his throat. She was alive, but this was far from over.

"I've got you, Jane. I've got you."

SOFT PULSES OF sound echoed in her ears. Her eyelids felt heavy, like she could sleep for a few more hours. But that beeping...

Jane ran her tongue across her bottom lip. Dry.

Cracking her eyes, she fought against the sudden onslaught of the fluorescent overhead lighting. She blinked to clear her head. White walls. White floors. White bedding. And an IV in her forearm. A strained groan vibrated up her throat. A hospital.

"Hello, gorgeous." Elliot stepped into her clouded vision, a bright smile plastered on his face. "I was hoping you'd wake up on my watch. There's something about those few short seconds of watching someone realize they're not dead after all."

"Hi," she said, her voice gravelly. Putting her hand to her throat, she tried massaging the dryness away, but it hung tight. "When did you get released?"

"Here, this'll help." Handing her a clear cup of water with a straw, he helped her adjust to a sitting position and fluffed her pillows before she relaxed back into the bed. "I checked myself out as soon as I heard about what happened at the sheet metal factory. Couldn't sit there and let you and Sullivan have all the fun."

"Yeah, fun." Stinging pain radiated across her shoulders as she struggled to sit up, and she wrenched forward with a hiss. She angled her head over her shoulder. White gauze and tape covered the burns under the thin hospital gown, but she was all too aware of how they'd gotten there in the first place. Christopher Menas. The sheet metal factory. The helicopter. And Sullivan. She scanned the room for those sea-blue eyes, but her stomach sank. "How long have I been out?"

She took a long, slow sip of water. Her muscles relaxed as the liquid did its job in her throat, and Jane set her head back against the pillows. Couldn't have been more than a day or two, right? Where did that leave them? "Is Christopher dead? Is it over?"

"Not by a long shot, beautiful. But come on now." Elliot sat in a padded chair he'd pulled next to the bed and laced his fingers behind his head, still smiling. He looked awfully chipper for someone who'd had his head nearly smashed in by a tow-truck-operator-turned-mercenary. "You know that's not what you want to ask me."

She didn't dare ask about Sullivan. Asking meant she'd be breaking one of her own rules that she'd set when she'd decided to blackmail a former navy SEAL: no getting emotionally attached. "How long have I been out?"

"Two days," Elliot said.

Inhaling some of the water, Jane coughed and spit until she cleared her lungs.

Elliot shot forward and took the cup from her, as she covered her mouth with one of the sheets. Sitting back down, he waited until she took a full breath, then sat forward. His deep brown eyes studied her, that infectious smile gone. "He knows what you did, Jane, offering yourself up as bait. He found the camera in your room."

"Oh." She sat back again, swiping one hand through her short hair and running the edge of her sheet under her fingernail with the other. She focused on the bedding and not the disappointment in Elliot's eyes. Why she cared to give Sullivan's private investigator an explanation, she had no idea. But the words fell from her mouth anyway. "We were out of leads, and

I needed to know who was doing this to me. It didn't make sense that Christopher might be stalking me all these years later. I'm not a threat to him anymore. The statute of limitations ran out a year ago." She took a deep breath to counteract the painful reminder of her and Christopher's reunion at the factory. "There's something else going on here. Menas said something…" A headache pounded at the base of her skull. "But I can't remember what."

"Elliot, get out," a familiar voice commanded from the door.

"Sullivan." Jane shot her head up. The dread that'd pooled at the base of her spine spread thin, and she straightened a bit more. Pure rage tightened the small muscles controlling his expression, and he suddenly seemed much more dangerous than she remembered. Didn't matter. He was here. He was okay.

"Hey, look at that, my shift is over. By the way, I've been eating your chocolate pudding for the last two days. I'll pay you back when you're out of here." Elliot somehow gracefully maneuvered around his boss and escaped down the hall as though he'd done this before.

And by the serious lines carved into Sullivan's features, Jane bet he had.

Seconds ticked by, possibly minutes. She

couldn't tell. One part of her wished Sullivan would step completely into her room and help her forget the horrible memories of the past few days. The other part demanded she keep her head on straight and remember why she'd blackmailed him in the first place. To bring her stalker to justice.

"You could've been killed." He rolled his fingers into fists. "You almost were."

And he'd been hurt by the look of his arms and knuckles. The air rushed out of her as she scanned the cuts and bruises marring his tanned skin. Christopher Menas had gotten in a few good hits. Because of her. She'd screwed up any chance of catching her stalker by running out her front door without any idea of what waited on the other side. "Sullivan, I'm sorry. I had no idea Christopher would have backup—"

"That's right. You had no idea. We were supposed to investigate the leads together, Jane, but this is what I find instead." He shoved a hand into his jeans pocket and tossed the small camera she'd mounted in her room onto the bed. Broken into several pieces. "You put me and my entire team at risk by going after Menas yourself."

Jane didn't know what else to say, her throat closing as she fought to hold on to the last remnants of her emotional control. She fisted her hands in the sheets. Rolling her lips between her teeth, she bit down to stay in the moment. She couldn't fight Christopher and his team of mercenaries on her own, but she hadn't meant to put the Blackhawk Security team's lives at stake either. They deserved more. Sullivan deserved more. "You're right. I wasn't thinking clearly."

He stalked toward her like a soldier, his grip loose at his sides, ready to go for his weapon at a moment's notice. He walked with power. The edge of her mattress dipped under his weight, his body heat tunneling through the sheets on her bed and down into her bones. Jane couldn't think about her awareness of him right now. Because something had changed. He was looking at her differently. Like he actually would've cared had Christopher gotten her onto that helicopter. "Do you know what would've happened if Menas had killed you?"

The memories flooded in with no one to stop them from overtaking the small amount of control she'd built up. Jane blinked back the tears welling in her lower eyelids. "Well, you definitely wouldn't have had to worry about me blackmailing you anymore."

"That's not my priority right now, Jane.

You're a survivor. Like me. Setting up the camera, going after Menas…" He exhaled hard. "As much as I want to be angry at you for it, you did what you felt like you had to do, and I respect you for it. You're strong, you're used to taking care of yourself, but you hired me to protect you, and I can't do that when you're running your own agenda on the side. Understand?" He slid his fingers into her hair, caging her between his massive calloused palms. Those mesmerizing blue eyes bored deep down into her as though he could bare every inch of her with a single look. Sullivan's tone dipped into dangerous territory. "If Menas had gotten you onto that helicopter, I would've spent the rest of my life hunting him and every associate involved until I put them all in the ground."

She blinked to restart her circuits. "I've upended your entire life. Twice. Why would you care what happens to me?"

"Because you put aside your own well-being to save my and Elliot's lives." Sullivan dropped the pad of his thumb to the crack in her bottom lip, and something hot and sensual rushed through her. He thought all that about her? "And because Menas won't stop coming after you, and I'm eager to personally introduce him to a world of disappointment."

He housed shadows—downright darkness sometimes—but he was also honorable. He gave his word and followed through. More than she could say about any other man in her life.

"You think highly of yourself, don't you?" And with damn good reason. SEALs were the principal special operators of the navy. With sea, land and air in their blood, they could operate in any kind of environment, hostile or not. The edges of his dark trident tattoo peeked out from under his T-shirt sleeve. Dryness set up residence in her throat again, and it had nothing to do with the drugs the hospital staff had given her over the last two days. But she sobered almost instantly. "Everyone who gets close to me ends up hurt. All my friends…my family."

No one had understood why she hadn't come back from college the same, why she couldn't move on from what Christopher had done. She didn't have anyone left.

"Then it's a good thing I can take care of myself." Sullivan set one hand beside her hip and leaned in, totally and completely focused on her. He teased her senses in every possible way. His fingertips streaking softly down her bruised jawline, his clean, masculine scent filling her lungs, the sound of his uneven breathing. Every cell in her body stood at attention, wanting him to kiss her, needing him. He traced over the cuts along her arms and collarbone, then pulled away. Air rushed from her lungs, her head clearing fast. "Menas is going to pay. I promise. I have Anthony tracking his movements since his team pulled him off the highway as we speak. We're going after him."

She didn't want to think about that right now, not with him this close, not with him chasing back the pain her body still clung to. Then his words registered. Wait. What? Jane straightened, the burns along her shoulder blades pulling a hiss from her lips. "Sullivan—"

"That's not my name." He pulled away, but the remnants of his touch would stick with her long after they finished their investigation and went their separate ways. "I want to hear my real name on your lips. I need to hear you say it, just once."

Her brows drew inward. "But you're not that man anymore."

"You don't know that," he said. "You don't know anything about me."

A weak smile pulled at the corners of her mouth. If this was some kind of test, proof that she knew who he was and what he'd done, Sullivan Bishop was in for a rude awakening. "All right, *Sebastian Warren*, you want to go after Menas? Fine. But you're taking me with you."

## Chapter Nine

Another Fine Navy Day.

Or, in other words, not so much.

Sullivan rolled his head back, stretching the stiff muscles in his neck. The second trip to the cabin hadn't been nearly as exciting as the first. Of course, had Jane been *his* target, he would've struck while she lay unconscious in the hospital. But Menas had to be licking some wounds right about now. His attention drifted to the closed bedroom door. Jane had taken the single bedroom in order to clean up and rest, but he couldn't sleep.

Not with an entire group of mercenaries coming after her.

The stitches in his upper arm stretched as he pushed himself off the couch for yet another perimeter check. He wasn't taking any chances this time. The investigation had gone from gathering intel on a tow truck operator who couldn't let the past die to defending Jane against an armored attack. Sullivan parted the blinds hanging in the front window, his favorite Glock in hand. The gun wasn't his only line of defense this time. He'd made sure Anthony had visited over the last few days to turn the cabin from his getaway spot to a fortified bunker. If Menas and his band of mercenaries came within a hundred yards of the cabin, Sullivan would know.

"Couldn't sleep?" Her husky voice straightened his spine. Those hazel eyes brightened as Sullivan looked her over in the overlarge T-shirt and sweatpants he'd lent her from his dresser drawers. His private investigator had dropped off a duffel bag of clothing and shoes for her but had somehow "forgotten" Jane's sleepwear. Her long fingers stretched around the mug of coffee he'd made her when they'd first arrived. She was the epitome of perfection—more beautiful than he'd imagined—and his mouth went dry. "Me neither."

Sullivan cleared his throat. "How are you feeling?"

"Everything hurts and I'm dying." A rush of laughter burst from her chest, but she grabbed for her bruised jaw. The swelling had gone down, but the pain obviously hadn't subsided just yet. Even so, her smile warmed parts of

Sullivan he'd almost forgotten existed. Flashes of threading his fingers through her hair, of bringing that delectable mouth to his, streaked through his mind. "But I can't complain too much. I'm alive, right?"

Thank heaven for that. "It wouldn't bother me if you did." Sullivan replaced the gun in his shoulder holster and rested his hands at his sides. "You've been through a lot the past few days."

"We both have." Setting the mug on the countertop to her left, Jane tucked her short hair behind her ears. Her lean frame drowned in his clothes, but something deep inside him wouldn't dream of dressing her in anything else. Because as he'd watched Menas haul her toward that chopper, he'd realized just how far he was willing to go to keep her safe. She'd gone up against a mercenary alone. And survived. How many of Christopher Menas's victims could say the same?

"Sullivan, listen." One hand leveraged on the counter, the other on her hip, Jane rolled her lips into her mouth, a tell, he'd noted, of when she was nervous. Her gaze rose to his, a hint of pink rising up her neck and into her cheeks. "I can't begin to tell you how sorry I am for what happened at my town house. The camera…" She shook her head, eyes closing briefly as though she could undo everything over the last two days. "It was stupid. The whole thing was stupid. I should've told you what I was doing." She centered on him. "I'm sorry I didn't trust you enough to tell you what I'd been planning. It won't happen again."

Sullivan's fingers twitched at his sides. He'd thought about that particular piece of information a lot over the course of the last two days as he and Elliot took apart Christopher Menas's cover piece by piece. She hadn't trusted him to get the job done, to protect her, but Sullivan wouldn't let the sting sink too deep. Despite her reputation, he saw her distrust for what it really was. Survival. Jane waited for his response, her teeth digging into that split bottom lip of hers. He'd tell her the truth. "If it hadn't been for you luring Menas in, we probably never would've uncovered his real profession."

"As a mercenary." The words left her mouth as a whisper, as though she couldn't believe her college boyfriend was so adept at violence.

"We confirmed it a little while ago. Makes sense when you think about it. You said it yourself. Christopher Menas likes to hurt people. He doesn't have any regard for authority and doesn't believe in the justice system. The sexual assault against your roommates while you two were in college was only the beginning." Sullivan had come across a few mercs during his time as a SEAL, had even been asked if he'd wanted to get in on the ground floor of a new private security company that specialized in Menas's kind of work not too long ago. His brother, Marrok, saw the career potential before he'd died—he swallowed back the tightness in his throat—but Sullivan only killed to survive or protect. Not for a paycheck. "Unfortunately, clients will pay a lot of money for traits like that."

"I take it since you've added a few new security measures to the cabin you still think he's a threat." Jane shifted on her feet. "You were going to kill him, weren't you? Even after I asked you to have him arrested and tried."

"Yes." Plain and simple. She'd asked for the justice system to punish Menas for his crimes, but in those rage-induced seconds of Sullivan fighting for his life—fighting for *hers*—he'd made a choice. He took a deep breath. "Men like Christopher Menas don't give up. They get off by making others suffer. I couldn't watch that happen to you."

"I understand." She ran a hand up and over her shoulder, where the worst of Menas's damage had been cleaned and bandaged. The burned skin would scar but could never detract from Jane's beauty. A weak smile sharpened the angles of her face. "I might not be able to sleep for a few days. But that's nothing new. Christopher's been stalking me for a while. I should be used to it, shouldn't I?"

Sullivan opened his mouth, wanting to assure her this was the safest place for her to be, that he could protect her from any kind of danger. But he had a sense the fears Jane talked about weren't entirely physical. And he could relate. The brightness in her gaze dimmed slightly, and he couldn't help but close the distance between them. He notched her chin higher to have her look straight at him. "When this is over, the nightmares will get better. It'll just take time."

He studied the slim navy-blue box on the bookshelf over her shoulder, the one with the custom-made pen he'd kept after all these years. A gift from his mother. Identical to the pen she'd given Marrok when he'd turned twelve. "Someday, you'll wake up and they won't be the first thing you think about in the morning. After that, you won't remember them."

"Was that how it was for you?" Nothing but the pure need of reassurance radiated in her eyes. "After what happened with your dad?"

Yes. Violence left a stain, one that took a long time to bleach out. That single incident at age fifteen had changed the course of his life. It'd taken every penny he owned to have a new identity forged. He'd had his birth name declared deceased and gone into the military a few years later, desperate to get away. Joined the SEALs. Founded Blackhawk Security. Dropping his hand to his side, Sullivan focused on the warm, far too intelligent woman in front of him. He wasn't about to tell that particular story. Because it wouldn't end the way she hoped. "You should eat something. Get some rest. We have a lot of work ahead of us."

He turned away.

"You asked me to call you Sebastian in the hospital. Right after you…" She inhaled sharp and clear, the feeling of his hands on her smooth skin still so clear. "Do you remember that?" Soft footsteps padded toward him, and before he was ready, she slid her long fingers over his bare arm to turn him around.

"I remember." He remembered everything since setting sights on her in that damn hospital bed. The way her eyes lit up at the sight of him. The way her lips had creased when he'd slipped his thumb over her mouth. The undeniable rage to tear Christopher Menas to pieces as he'd traced her injuries. Another round of tension stiffened his muscles. No man had the right to hit a woman, but Menas wasn't a real man. He was a gun for hire. Any kind of morality had gone out the window long before their run-in on Seward Highway.

Sullivan closed his eyes. Heat ran up his fingers and into his shoulders. His skin tingled where she touched him. Desire stirred in his gut, kicking up speed the longer Jane held on to him. He turned toward her, nothing but her vanilla scent in his lungs. How could she possibly still smell so good after what she'd been through? "You think I'm not that man anymore."

"Am I wrong?" Jane maneuvered her hand over his chest, her heat tunneling through his T-shirt and down beneath his sternum. Down to the spot where his soul resided. "I read the papers. I know you were only a teenager when you—"

"Killed my father for murdering my mother and eleven other women?" There. He'd said it. He'd drawn blood at the tender age of fifteen and hadn't looked back. Not even for his younger brother. Sullivan squared his shoulders. "Release of that information might lose me the business I've built from the ground up, but the Anchorage Lumberjack was a serial killer who started with women who wouldn't agree to his advances and ended with my mother. So if you're looking for some kind of guilty plea, you're not going to find it, Counselor."

"I'm not looking for a guilty plea." Jane fanned her fingers over his chest. "I just want to get to know the man taking on an entire mercenary ring for me."

Get to know him? This woman wanted to face off with years of his personal demons? A laugh rumbled deep in his chest. Having her this close, with nothing but honesty and desire in her expression, Sullivan couldn't back away. As he should. Never mind that she'd blackmailed him into this mess in the first place, but Jane had single-handedly brought down the only family he'd had left.

But she hadn't forced his brother to commit suicide, had she? Marrok had pulled the trigger himself. And the blackmail... Well, he was a SEAL, damn it. He had held live grenades in his bare hands, had prevented an attack on civilians in the Middle East, could hold his breath for more than three minutes without releasing a single bubble underwater. Blackmail didn't compare to the last twelve years of nonstop training and missions he'd successfully completed. If anyone could battle the monsters hiding in his closet, the Full Metal Bitch had the best chance of survival. "Are you sure you can handle it?"

"I've faced dangerous, military-trained criminals every day of my career, survived two attempts on my life by a mercenary and dragged your deadweight through the Alaskan wilderness by myself." Her mouth turned up into a gut-wrenching smile that clenched his insides and destroyed his excuses. "Why don't you give me a challenge?"

WHY DID HER heart insist on getting involved in things it had no business interfering with? Its job was to pump blood. That was it. Get to know the real Sullivan Bishop? That should've been the last thing on her mind. But at the moment, Jane couldn't remember why. His eyes had settled on her, and the pain, the exhaustion, the alarm bells sounding off in her head all disappeared.

He shouldn't have touched her in the hospital. Because now all she could think about was having those hands on her again. And, hell, if that didn't send her thoughts on tangents everywhere but where it should be: on bringing her stalker to justice.

The shadows across the rough ridge of his nose shifted as Sullivan closed in on her. The action, so simple, set off an explosive chain reaction that stole the air from her lungs. Skin heated, heart racing, her fight-or-flight response kicked into high gear. He'd almost kissed her back in the hospital, but this, the desire raging in his gaze, was something completely different. Like he'd finally come to a decision about her.

Long-dormant longing flooded through her, but she stepped out of Sullivan's range. She had been fed, had rested, felt safe here in his cabin, everything that said she was supposed to be ready for an intimate relationship according to Maslow's hierarchy of needs, but she couldn't do this. At least, not with him.

Take care of the threat. Get her life back.

Mind over matter. That was all it'd take.

They'd only known each other for four days—albeit four of the most intense days of her life—but people got hurt when they insisted on staying in her life.

"Jane?" Confusion chased the desire from his expression. "What's wrong?"

Good question. She'd been with a handful of men in the past. Nothing serious. But it was like riding a bike, right? Except this bike was inexplicably protective of her, had taken on a group of mercenaries to save her life and stared at her as though he intended to devour her. Sullivan was a good man. And despite her original intentions when she'd broken into his office, she wouldn't let him throw away his life for her. Because guilt was the unwanted gift that just kept on giving.

"Everything." Jane ran a hand through her hair, then crossed her arms over her stomach and leaned against the back of the couch for support. Her knees locked to keep her upright when all she wanted to do was collapse into Sullivan. All the oxygen disappeared from the room. The three small lines between his eyebrows deepened, and she clenched her jaw to keep herself in the moment. Why was her chest so tight? "I blackmailed you into helping me, Sullivan, but after what happened with Christopher... I have no idea how to get you out of this."

"Get me out of this?" Sullivan widened his stance, crossing his arms over his chest. "What gave you the idea I'm looking for a way out?"

"You beat Christopher Menas until he was unconscious to save me on the highway. In my experience, mercenaries like him aren't going to forget about something like that and move on. He's turned you into a target, too." She inhaled deep, savoring his masculine, clean scent. "I know what you said about taking care of yourself before, but people who've gotten close to me over the years always end up hurt. And for some stupid reason, I don't want that to happen to you."

Silence stretched between them, a living, breathing thing.

Slowly, dangerously, Sullivan stalked toward her, a predator closing in on his prey. Before Jane had a chance to escape, he caged her between his massive arms against the couch, just as he had back in his office. The ice in his gaze melted, warming every inch of her body. "Do I look like the kind of man who's willing to back down from a fight?"

Not in the least.

"Stop looking at me like that." Jane straightened—at a loss with him practically wrapped around her—but she didn't get far. Didn't he understand? Nothing could happen between them. Ever. Christopher wasn't going to stop. He'd hunt her down until he got whatever kind of revenge he sought from her. There was nowhere she could go that didn't put them both in danger. Clearing her throat, she stood up against him. Fine. He wouldn't back down voluntarily? She'd make him see reason. "You should hate me for what happened with your brother, for what I did to force you to help me."

"I tried. It didn't work." The cage he'd constructed around her disappeared. The muscles in the right side of his jaw ticked off a steady beat. "Do you want me to hate you? Is that it?"

It would sure make them going their separate ways easier after they finished with Christopher and his friends. But what if they never found him? She'd have to leave her job with the JAG Corps. Change her name. Move again. Jane exhaled hard, but the tightness in her chest didn't lessen. What if her stalker got to her again and Sullivan wasn't around the next time? Rapid flashes of what'd happened in the factory took over, and the burns across her back tingled. Without Sullivan, who knew what would've happened to her had Christopher gotten her onto that chopper. Dread curdled in her gut. She didn't want to think about it.

"We've gone up against some of the most violent men in existence, Jane. Men most people would run from. But you...you held your ground. You've fought like hell for yourself and for me since you broke into my office." Sullivan stared down at her. "You might be the Full Metal Bitch, but I can't hate you."

Her insides warmed, relaxing her muscles.

This should've been easy. She'd planned everything down to the letter. She'd blackmail him into tracking down her stalker, the police would take over and she'd have her life back. Sullivan wasn't supposed to take on a clan of mercenaries for her. She wasn't supposed to consider what might happen to them after the job was done.

Oh, no. No, no, no, no. She did not have feelings for him. She couldn't. First rule of blackmail: don't fall in love.

Jane inhaled deep, swiping her tongue across her bottom lip. Her heart pounded loud in her ears. She couldn't get enough air. She took a deep breath to steady her nerves, but it didn't help. "Then where does that leave us?"

"Jane, my brother made his own choices. I honestly don't know what kind of man Marrok turned out to be, or whether or not he assaulted those women, but I do know you. I left that life behind—I left him behind—and while I will regret that for the rest of my life, I have every reason to believe you did your job." Wrapping his strong, calloused fingers around her upper arms, Sullivan slid his thumbs over her skin in comforting circles. Goose bumps prickled down her arms, the combination of cold and hot fighting for her senses. "You might've brought up the charges against Marrok, but nobody forced him to eat his gun. And—" his wide, muscled chest expanded on a deep inhale "—from what I've learned about you over the last few days, I don't think you'd do something like that without cause."

Jane blinked. "You don't?"

"No," he said. "Because we're a team, and I do everything in my power to back up the people on my team. And if you can believe it, that even includes Elliot." His smile vaporized the knot of apprehension that had set up shop in her chest.

Jane sank into him, setting her ear against Sullivan's chest. The steady thump of his heart settled her fried nerve endings, but the silence before the storm wouldn't last long. Christopher was still out there, still hunting her. Sullivan slid his hands up her back, thankfully avoiding the burns across her shoulder blades. "Someday, when all this is over, you're going to have to tell me what Elliot did to land in your good graces."

"Only if you tell me how you got into my office." He set his lips against the crown of her head.

"Did you think it would be that easy?" A laugh escaped from between her lips. How could she have wanted to push Sullivan away?

The man was a SEAL for crying out loud. He took on the most dangerous threats to the United States with green paint on his face and a motto on his lips.

All in, all the time. For her.

# Chapter Ten

Splashes of pinks, greens and purples wove intricate designs overhead. Aurora borealis. One of the most beautiful things he'd had the privilege of experiencing in his life. But nothing compared to the woman next to him. Three days ago, she'd survived what would probably be the most brutal attack of her life, yet here she sat, stunning as ever.

Puffs of air crystallized in front of his mouth as Sullivan exhaled. The temperature had dropped significantly over the last fifteen minutes, but he didn't dare move. Not with those vibrant colors lighting up the snow before the heavy tree line, and not with Jane bundled this close into his side.

"I've never seen the northern lights this clearly before." A fresh mug of steaming coffee gripped in her hand, she stared up at the sky. Her pupils lit up as the shifts in color played across her face. She huddled deeper into her coat, setting her head against his shoulder. "Never thought I'd get the chance to sit here and enjoy it. It's nice."

Sullivan took a sip of his own black coffee, every high-strung muscle relaxing one by one. There was something about watching the northern lights, enjoying a cup of coffee, feeling a woman's heartbeat against his side that washed the tightness from his chest. When was the last time that'd happened? A year? Two? A decade? There'd been women. Nothing serious. But this—*Jane*—was different.

The Glock he'd strapped under his jacket pressed into him. Well, he wasn't completely relaxed. Menas could show up uninvited anytime, but the merc wouldn't touch another hair on Jane's head. Ever. Sullivan's gaze followed a line of bright pink up and over the thick tree line surrounding his property. "I come out here when I need to get away from everything and everyone, or my back needs actual support from a bed instead of my office sofa night after night. Clears my head." A smile tugged at one corner of his mouth as he took another drink of his coffee. This cabin had saved his life and his sanity more than once over the years, given him the solitude he craved. He lowered his voice. "Now, if I could get rid of you, it'd be perfect."

The muscles around her spine tightened as she rammed her elbow back into his solar plexus, and Sullivan couldn't help but flinch. The woman was strong, a lot stronger than she looked, the kind of woman he'd be proud to have at his side in the middle of a fight. Jane tipped her head back to meet his eyes, a gutwrenching smile on her lips. "Tell more jokes like that. I've got all night."

"Jokes? What are you talking about? I was completely serious," he said.

"All right." Jane shoved away from him, hurrying across the snow-covered deck as flakes quickly replaced the ones her footsteps disrupted. Doubling over, she scooped up a handful of snow and packed it between her hands. "You want to play it that way? Let's do this."

She wound her arm back and let the snowball fly.

Sullivan saw it coming but couldn't move fast enough without spilling his coffee. He dived to the other side of the bench, but it was too late. Snow plastered against his neck and melted down into his heavy jacket, setting his skin on fire. Coffee surged over the edge of his mug and spilled down his jeans. A small growl reverberated through his chest. Slowly, carefully, he set the coffee down, stood and brushed off the remnants of pure white snow.

"Are you sure you want to go down this path, Captain?" Taking a single step forward, Sullivan mentally prepared his attack, always thinking ahead to the next move and the one after that. "Because I don't know if you're aware of this, but I've been known to handle myself in tough situations. Some fairly recently. And I wouldn't want you to get hurt."

"I played varsity softball in high school and college, even helped win the army's annual softball tournament while on tour. I think I can take care of myself." Jane tossed another ball of snow a few inches up in the air and caught it bare-handed. "Unless you're scared to take me on?"

"Oh, you're going down." Sullivan lunged.

Her eyes widened a split second before she turned tail and ran as fast as she could for the tree line. He appreciated the view as high-pitched laughter drifted over the deep snowbanks she tried plowing through, but Jane couldn't outrun him. Hour after hour, he'd trained in this forest, mentally mapped out every tree, every rock, anywhere the enemy could hide. She didn't have a chance. Snow kicked up around her as she darted toward the trees, and time seemed to slow.

All his life he'd fought for control. Relentless command over his body, his mind, his life. Growing up in a psychopath's house demanded nothing less, especially for Marrok's sake. But it was the military that had beat self-reliance into him. Nobody would control him, no one would hurt him like his father had hurt their family. But the warmth blossoming in his chest right now wasn't under his control. The second Jane had broken into his office, something had changed.

Four days. That was all it'd taken for her to melt his steel heart. Saving his life in the wilderness, putting her own at risk for Elliot when the fire broke out in Menas's apartment... None of it had lined up with her reputation. Could've been intentional, Jane's way of going the extra mile to secure his services, but Sullivan's instincts said that side of her never really existed in the first place. It'd been her defense mechanism, just as solitude had been his. Sullivan took a deep breath. Dozens of men had tried to stop his heart, but Jane could actually hurt him.

The thought knotted a tight fist of anxiety in his chest, but that didn't stop Sullivan from balling a handful of snow and nailing Jane in the middle of the back. The stitches in his arm stretched, but he pushed the discomfort to the back of his mind. She'd started this fight, he'd finish it. Sullivan bent over to gather more snow, but when he'd straightened, Jane had disappeared.

The smile pulling at his mouth vanished. Dead silence surrounded him, the tree line clear. He struggled to level out his racing heartbeat but took a deep breath. Vanilla infused the light breeze cutting through the trees. She hadn't gone far. Darting for the patch of snow he'd last seen her, Sullivan tracked a set of footsteps toward the tree line. If Menas had gotten a hold of her...

A wall of coat-padded woman tackled him to the ground.

His heart rocketed into his throat as Jane's soft groan transformed into a trail of laughter and eased the tension hardening his muscles. He stared up at her, those sharp features surrounded by pinks, greens and blues in the dancing night sky. How had she managed to sneak up on him like that? He was a SEAL. Nothing got past him.

"Easy there, soldier. You don't want to make any sudden moves." Straddling him, Jane raised a snow-filled hand. Her smile lit up his insides and chased the remnants of the small adrenaline rush from his veins. "This snowball is deadly cold, and I'm prepared to use it."

Scanning the spot where he'd seen her positioned last, Sullivan rested his head into the snow. The sensitive skin on the back of his neck burned as he fought to catch his breath. "Where the hell did you come from?"

"Sneak attack from the trees." She'd lowered her voice as though she were telling him a secret, those perfect, kissable lips spread wide. Straightening, Jane washed the smile from her features. "Silence!"

Setting one hand on his chest, Jane let drops of melted snow fall against his neck. The beads of frigid water panicked his nervous system, and he struggled underneath Jane as though he couldn't bear the thought of torture. "I warned you, Sullivan Bishop. I am very good at this game and I'm serious about winning. Now, it's my turn to ask the questions."

An interrogation. Interesting.

"You got me. I'll tell you everything." Sullivan raised his hands in surrender, but with her strong thighs gripping his hips—every man's dream—he had no intention of cooperating with her demands. No. He was going to drag this out as long as he could.

"Good. And you shall be rewarded for your cooperation." She tossed the snowball to the ground and fitted her hand around his neck. Cold penetrated deep under his jacket as she leaned in close, her lips mere inches from his, but Sullivan didn't dare move. "Tell me, if you could go anywhere in the world right now, where would you go?"

He rested his palms on the tops of her knees, the denim covering her legs thin enough he could feel her body heat. The strong muscles under her clothing urged him to slide his hands higher, but Sullivan kept himself in control. He wasn't an animal. He wouldn't take until she offered. However long that might be. "I'd be stupid to move an inch right now."

"Yes, you would be, but that's not what I asked. And now you must be punished." The edges of her mouth turned upward, and before he understood what she'd meant, she held another handful of snow over his face and neck. Freezing water trailed under his coat and T-shirt, and Sullivan had had enough.

He maneuvered one foot behind hers and bucked with the opposite hip. Jane fell to the side, and he rolled on top of her, pinning her into the snow. He was back in control. And she was his. Snowflakes peppered their clothing, but soon they'd be too cold to do anything but run for the closest hot shower. Maybe together. He held his weight off her, careful of her wounds, grip loose around her wrists, giving her the chance to escape if she wanted. But the surprised look in those hazel eyes said she planned on staying right where she was. "Now it's my turn to ask the questions."

"All right," she said. "Shoot."

"Are you going back into the army when this investigation is over?" He shouldn't have asked, didn't have any right, but Sullivan hadn't been able to think of anything else since he'd checked her out of the hospital a few hours ago.

Any evidence of playfulness disappeared from her features. "I haven't thought about it. After what happened at the factory, I didn't think I'd make it out alive."

Nothing but their combined breathing filled the silence, as a fresh wave of snow fell from the sky. Hell. He hadn't meant to resurrect those memories. The past few minutes with her had put them, and the man responsible, to the back of his mind. Freeing him from responsibility, revenge, rage. Sullivan lightened his hold on her and pulled back to give her some room.

"You are not what has happened to you,

Jane." He tamped down on the strange ache growing in the middle of his chest. Sullivan had never been the relationship type, but right now, with Jane pinned underneath him, he could see himself following her down that path when this was over. If she let him. Because the thought of losing her in the middle of that highway had nearly killed him. "You're what you choose to become. Remember that."

Her mouth parted, breathing slightly uneven. "Are we really going after Christopher?"

"I like to finish what I start," he said.

Jane pushed her weight onto her elbows to sit up, with him still straddled across her legs. A shiver rode across her chest. "Do you think we'll survive?"

"I don't know." Better to tell her the truth, but as her features fell, Sullivan let the urge to protect her rage through him. His hands fisted in her thick jacket, pulling her toward him. "But I'm sure as hell not going down without a fight."

SULLIVAN BISHOP WASN'T the knight in shining armor, the one who had never been to war. He was the knight with tarnished and dented armor who knew how to win the fight and keep her safe. He'd taken Christopher and his band of mercenaries down once before. He could do it again.

But what if he couldn't or, worse, didn't survive?

Her gaze snapped to his. Jane clenched her jaw, refusing to let her thoughts sprint down that path. Because, if she was completely honest with herself, she'd rather run from Christopher for the rest of her life than let Sullivan become another casualty in this mess.

"Jane?" Concern deepened his tone.

Forget the frigid temperatures and the falling snow. Her body urged her to close the small space between them. She wanted to kiss him. More than wanted. *Needed* to. Puffs of frozen air solidified in front of her mouth. And the longer Jane studied his shadow of a beard, the sea-blue eyes that revealed his true intensions, the way his forehead creased when he was thinking something over, that need strengthened. "Don't talk. Just…"

Heat spread behind her sternum, lifting her up, pressing her against him. The burns across her back protested, but the dull sting wouldn't stop her. Only the sound of their combined exhales reached her ears, her heartbeat steady, calm. Cold seeping through her jeans demanded her attention, but anticipation for the feeling of his lips against hers—of finally tasting him—drowned out her body's survival instincts.

Sullivan's patience disappeared.

Gripping the back of her neck, he crushed his mouth to hers. The cold reaching down into her bones melted away as the rich taste of him spread across her tongue. Black coffee, peppermint and something smoother. Like a dark scotch. The elaborate combination heightened her senses to another level. The pressure at the back of her neck lightened, but Jane didn't move away. Tilting her head to the side, she opened wider for him, invited him to take more. Take all of her.

But Sullivan took his time. Nibbling, nuzzling, going slow. So slow. Her insides flooded with need as he nipped at her bottom lip, a spike of desire rushing through her blood. He threaded his fingers through the nap of hair at the base of her neck, pulling her harder against him. Her nerve endings fired in little electric pulses each time his lips moved against hers. The aurora above her, the snow below her, Sullivan around her. Jane never wanted to move.

But the Alaskan wilderness wasn't kind.

A shiver chased across her skin, and Sullivan pulled away. A burst of laughter rumbled deep in his chest. Didn't matter she'd worn her thickest coat from the duffel bag Elliot had dropped off. He ran his palms up and down her arms to generate some heat. "You're freezing."

Danger loomed ahead, but the man straddling her in the middle of his snow-covered property smiled. Her heart rate kicked up, and it had nothing to do with her mind telling her this couldn't happen. Sullivan Bishop, former navy SEAL burdened with years of death and destruction, looked happy for the first time since Jane had broken into his office. Melted snow had penetrated through her clothing but, in that moment, she didn't care. The world had changed. He'd changed. And she couldn't help but smile back. "I don't know how. You're like a furnace. Your body heat could keep us both alive for days."

"Yeah, but it was yours that kept me alive out here the first time." He pushed to his feet, offering her a hand to help her up. "Which I intend to repay you for."

"You've saved my life plenty since I pulled you out of the snow." She reached for him without hesitation, sliding her fingers across his calloused palms. Not harsh, but worked. Like him. The colors of the northern lights blended together as Sullivan pulled her into his chest, but they bled into the dark night sky the longer they stood together. Mother Nature's show had faded, but Jane would never forget these last few minutes. Never forget Sullivan when this ended. She fingered the zipper on his dark coat. "But if you want to pay me back, I have a couple things in mind."

Jane tugged on his jacket until his mouth met hers once again. She wasn't gentle. She wasn't careful. She meant to conquer, to banish the last few days. Pushing every bullet missed, every patch of skin burned, every second she felt like she was being watched into her kiss, Jane reveled in the feeling of lightness overwhelming her body. She breathed easier, sinking into Sullivan as she broke their connection. "That is, if you're up for it."

"I have a lot of unchecked frustration built up from the last few days. You might be the perfect person to help with that." The predatory desire raging in his eyes bolted straight to her core. Another round of heated arousal flooded her system as Sullivan wrapped his large hand around hers and tugged her after him. Snow kicked up into her boots, but Jane didn't slow as they vaulted up the front porch stairs.

A wall of warm air slammed into her, and Sullivan kicked the door closed behind them. Then his hands were on her. Pulling down the zipper on her coat, shoving the thick layers to the floor. His coat fell next, as Jane kicked off her boots, lost in his masculine scent, the mountain that was his rock-solid body. Her heart pounded loud in her ears, but nothing like in the factory as she'd run for her life. She was safe here. Sullivan was safe.

"You should get out of those wet clothes." He dropped his mouth to her neck, licking, nipping, hiking her arousal to levels she'd never experienced before. Her insides burned, every inch of her skin aware of only one thing: him.

But Jane planted her hand on his chest. All of this, the northern lights, the snowball fight, the kiss, it was everything she could hope for. But what about when it was over? Her leave was due to end in a week, and Sullivan had a business—a team—to run. Neither of those things left much room to explore this beyond tonight, but maybe that didn't have to be a bad thing. Maybe it was for the best. Because no matter how many people she'd cut herself off from, those who got close to her always ended up getting hurt. She stared straight up at him, almost a foot shorter but determined to hold her ground. "Before we do this, I need to know something."

"Ask me." He slid his hand over hers, his calluses scraping against her oversensitized skin.

Sincerity cooled the flood of desire in his gaze. "I'll tell you anything you want to know. No more secrets between us. I trust you."

"You do?" Her throat went dry, but the steady thump of his heart against her hand chased the surprise to the back of her mind.

"Yes." Sullivan stared down at her hand on his chest, stroking the back of her hand with his fingers. "You might've blackmailed me into helping you, but I'm glad you did." A laugh rumbled under her hand, and Jane couldn't help but smile. "I can't remember the last time I felt this good." His hand on her hip pinned her in place. "You already know my secrets. I don't have to hide from you like I do from my team. I don't have to be so controlled. It's…freeing."

The backs of her knees weakened, and Jane fisted his shirt to keep her balance. "Wow. You really know how to sweep a woman off her feet."

"That's the plan." A gut-twisting smile deepened the laugh lines around his mouth. Sullivan spread his fingers across the bare skin beneath her T-shirt. His touch battled the waves of debilitating coldness and won. In seconds, he'd warmed her more than an hour-long hot shower ever could have. "But what did you need to ask me?"

Ask him? Right. Shaking her head, Jane fought to focus over the desperate urge to mold herself to him. She pulled her bottom lip between her teeth, that knot of concern holding her tight. People might've gotten hurt because of her in the past, but Sullivan had made it perfectly clear he could take care of himself, had even proved it over the last few days. So maybe letting herself have feelings for the former navy SEAL she'd blackmailed wouldn't get him killed.

Jane checked the distance to the single bathroom over her shoulder, then turned back to him. "I need to know how long it's going to take for you to get me into a hot shower."

Faster than she thought possible, Sullivan buried his forearms behind her knees and lifted her into his arms without regard for the stitches in his arm. The cabin blurred in her vision, but he remained steady, a constant. The warm swirl of desire in his eyes tightened Jane's hold on his T-shirt. "Why don't we find out?"

## Chapter Eleven

Jane was asleep in his arms. Warm. Soft. Everything he'd ever imagined when he'd let his mind go down that path. Hope. Unquenched desire. And more. But the sun climbing over the Chugach Mountains claimed his attention. Sullivan dropped his nose to the crown of her head and breathed deep. Last night had been perfect in every regard, but, unfortunately, they were out of time.

He reached for his phone on the nightstand and swiped his thumb across the screen. A knot of tension chased back the peace running through his veins. The latest surveillance from Anthony and Elliot revealed Menas and his mercenaries gearing up in an abandoned construction site just outside the city. Sullivan knew the area but flicked through the brief's attached photos and the official report of Menas's history anyway. After skipping bail for the assault of three women in college, the seasoned hunter had realized he could make a living off doing what he did best: inflicting pain. Anthony's report started with a few jobs Menas had picked up working security for a Seattle company under an assumed name, then sped through the mercenary's climb to the private sector. From there, the money got better, the guns got bigger and Menas had put together his own team of mercenaries.

Right now, he had a team of three remaining, including himself, all highly armed with military-grade weapons and gear. Then again, the chopper landing in the middle of Seward Highway had already given Sullivan a clue. He dropped the phone to the sheets as Jane shifted in his arms, careful not to wake her. He'd had run-ins with mercs before, but not a single one of them had access to the kind of gear Menas had strapped to his hunting party. Despite not having anything to do with the military, Menas must have some kind of inside connection. Because stealing that grade of weapons and ammunition took a lot of bullets and skills that Sullivan would've heard of before now.

*Something else must be going on here.* Maybe Jane had been right back in the hospital. The statute of limitations to prosecute Menas for sexual assault had run out in the state of Washington several months ago, which meant the mercenary had no reason to come after her now.

Unless Menas and his team were only doing something that they'd been hired to do.

"How long do we have before we have to get out of bed?" The huskiness in Jane's sleep-filled voice raised the hairs on the back of his neck. Along with other things. Her fingers trailed across his chest, resurrecting overused nerve endings and sending a shiver across his chest. There was nothing like her touch. No one had brought his body to the brink over and over again like she had.

He pressed a kiss to her forehead, raptured with those hazel eyes staring up at him. Checking his phone again, he hit the silence button and rolled into her. "We have about fifteen minutes before Elliot walks through the front door."

"Mmm." Jane pressed her lips to his. The kiss was oddly sweet and full of promises he'd die trying to keep. He'd never been the sweet type. But promises? He intended to live up to every single one of them. For her. She maneuvered on top of him, chest to chest, the wrinkled sheets bunching over the small of her back. Soft skin surrounded him from almost every angle, and Sullivan wouldn't budge an inch. Dropping her chin to his sternum, she smiled. "Tell me he doesn't have a key and we can stretch those fifteen minutes out as long as possible."

For the first time in longer than Sullivan could remember, he laughed openly. Wrapping the top of his foot around hers, Sullivan flipped her onto her back and tossed his phone to the floor. He intended to bury himself in her warmth all over again, kissing her with everything he had left. "He most certainly does not have a key."

"Good," she said.

Fifteen minutes later, pounding on the front door pulled Sullivan from heaven. He shoved his legs through his jeans and laced his feet into his boots, closing the door behind him as Jane dressed. His heartbeat returned to a steady rhythm the more he distanced himself from her. Damn, that woman could do things to him with a single look, but last night and this morning? She'd turned his brain to mush and him into a grinning idiot.

"Right on time, Elliot." *Unfortunately.* Sullivan ripped open the front door, every cell in his body running cold.

Elliot wasn't standing on his porch.

A solid kick to the stomach knocked Sullivan to the floor, but he rebounded fast as adrenaline dumped into his blood. He lunged for the Glock in the shoulder holster hanging off one of the dining table chairs. Two pricks of pain embedded into the muscles along his bare back, then fired with white-hot electricity. Soft clicking reached his ears as the Taser wiped out his central nervous system. His body spasmed, curling his toes in his boots and his fingers into his palms. Jaw clenched, Sullivan fought in vain to reach the gun as current after current of electricity washed over him. The spasms rolled him onto his back, but he failed to dislodge the Taser's probes.

Christopher Menas stalked through the door, two members of his team on his tail, weapons up and fingers on triggers. A cruel smile split open the slash Jane had cut into the mercenary's cheekbone, and Sullivan couldn't help but smile back. Must've hurt like hell. They fanned out into the living room. Searching. "Check the bedroom. She's in here somewhere."

Jane was smart. She would've heard the commotion and gone out the bedroom window as fast as possible. Seconds ticked by. One of Menas's teammates kicked in the bedroom door when he couldn't open it manually, but the resulting silence said there was no sign of Jane. Sullivan kept his attention on the lead mercenary, the uncontrollable spasms lessening. She'd gotten out of the cabin. Relief flooded through him, but it wasn't over. He'd give her the time she needed to escape. Even if she had to leave him behind.

Menas's expression hardened as he focused those dark eyes back onto Sullivan. The mercenary lunged, wrapping a strong hand around his throat, and brought Sullivan to his feet. The probes ripped from his skin as Menas discarded the Taser and replaced the weapon in his hand with the M16 slung over his shoulder. One pull of the trigger, and the best medical examiner in the world would have a difficult time identifying Sullivan's insides. "Where is she?"

"You know something? I'm glad you're armed this time." Sullivan knocked Menas's hand away from his throat and threw a punch right into that gash on his face. The merc doubled over; Menas's trigger finger was too twitchy. Bullets sprayed across the floor, up the far wall and straight through one of his men, who hit the floor. Sullivan kicked the M16 away, but a fist to the right side of his face forced his vision to go dark for a split second.

Another kick to the torso threw him out the open front door and down the two short stairs on the porch. Blistering cold spread across his bare chest as he hit the snow.

Menas charged full force and caught Sullivan around the ribs, hiking him up and over his shoulder.

Sullivan threw two elbows to the spine. Three. Menas dropped him. Clutching the mercenary's jacket, Sullivan pushed the bastard backward, aiming punches for Menas's kidneys along the way. Sullivan blocked the first attempt to knock him out, but not the second. He stumbled back, out of breath, as Menas took a second to compose himself. Snow kicked up around him, but he barely felt the temperatures now as anticipation pumped hard through his veins. The teammate Menas hadn't killed watched on from the porch, weapon aimed to finish the job in case his superior lost the fight. Because this was between him and Christopher Menas.

Menas rolled his fists in a circular motion as though he'd done a few rounds of illegal bare-knuckle boxing before becoming a gun for hire. Wouldn't surprise Sullivan. The mercenary came at him with a straight blow to the head, which Sullivan blocked with his forearm, spinning his attacker ninety degrees and shooting an elbow straight into the back of Menas's knee. The mercenary's screams filled the small clearing as Menas shifted most of his weight to the opposite leg.

Time to end this.

"I warned you not to come after her, Menas." Sullivan clutched the mercenary's jacket, lining him up as he pulled back his elbow for one last hit. Jane wanted her stalker turned over to the authorities, but there was no stopping men like Christopher Menas. He leaned over his attacker. "You should've listened."

"My man over there will shoot you the second my heart stops beating. Then he'll go after Jane." The mercenary stared up at him. A line of blood dripped from his bottom lip but didn't stop him from pulling his mouth up into another crooked smile. "Is that what you want?"

Sullivan glanced toward the assault rifle targeted at him. "Doesn't matter what I want anymore. You went after Jane and tried to kill me in the process. No one is going to remember your name when you're dead."

A glint of sunlight flashed off the blade cutting toward him. Menas moved fast, faster than Sullivan thought possible after the energy they'd both expended, and sliced through muscle along his side. Searing pain spread across the left side of Sullivan's body. Blood seeped down into the waistband of his jeans and stained the bright white snow around him.

Repositioning the blade in his hand, Menas hiked himself higher in order to stab down at him. Sullivan crossed his forearms, barely holding back the blade's tip from his face. Menas was strong, but Sullivan was stronger.

He threw a knee into the mercenary's midsection and watched as the blade landed in a snowbank a few feet away. "Any other surprises you want to try before I break your neck?"

Sullivan's breath heaved in and out of his lungs. He was losing too much blood to keep this up for long, but Menas wasn't recovering as quickly either.

"This isn't over with me, you know." Menas bent at the waist, holding his side. Most likely a few broken ribs. Maybe Sullivan was lucky enough one of them had punctured a lung. "I'm not the only one he hired."

Sullivan's heart stuttered. "What did you just say?"

The mercenary lunged again, and Sullivan widened his stance for the hit.

A single gunshot exploded in the small clearing.

Both Menas and Sullivan turned toward the

shooter across the property, as Menas's team-mate swung his assault rifle toward Jane.

"Get away from him, Christopher." She held Sullivan's favorite Glock straight up in the air, but, closing a few feet of space between them, she aimed straight for Menas. "This is between you and me."

HER WORDS SOUNDED a whole lot more confident than Jane felt. She held the gun steady, relying on the countless hours she'd forced herself to brush up on her skills at the range. Her heart drummed too fast in her chest. Muscle memory kicked in after a few heartbeats, but these were mercenaries she was dealing with. Not some muscled jock of an ex-boyfriend who hadn't been able to get over the past. He'd turned himself into a professional killer.

"Jane, what are you doing? Get out of here." Sullivan doubled over. Blood dripped from between his fingers on his left side. He was injured. Damn it. What had Christopher done to him? Her protector didn't stay down long. He raised that intense gaze to her, expression stone-like, the muscles in his jaw frozen. "Get out of here. *Now.*"

He was too stubborn and too strong.

But Jane wasn't going anywhere.

"Once again, the army is coming to bail the navy out of trouble." Not a time to make jokes, but her gut instincts were telling her all she needed to do here was stall. Elliot was on his way. Wasn't that what Sullivan had said earlier? She only hoped the private investigator had thought to bring backup.

"No," she continued. "I'm getting you out of this mess. Once and for all." She focused on Christopher. Sullivan had done his job. He'd found her stalker and she could take care of the rest. "Attempted murder. Stalking in the second degree. I could keep going. You have a lifetime of prison ahead of you, Christopher."

"Janey." Christopher limped two steps toward her, hands in the air as though he was about to surrender. Jane knew better. The last thing on the mercenary's mind was giving up. He took one more step. "We both know you're not going to shoot me. You're a lawyer, remember? Not a killer."

Jane dropped the gun a few inches and pulled the trigger. The bullet disappeared into the snow at Christopher's feet. "I might be a lawyer, but I still know how to use a gun." She directed him to the right. "Now, have your friend join you over there by Sullivan and drop your weapons."

Christopher's smile burned straight through her soul. Pure evil. "Janey—"

"Do it!" She fired another round near his right foot. Her hand tingled from the kickback, but Jane was prepared to fire a lot more shots if he forced her.

"Guess we've got to do what the lady says." Shrugging at his teammate, the mercenary tossed his remaining guns and blades into the snow at his feet and maneuvered closer to Sullivan. The second mercenary followed suit, losing his gun in the snow. "What now, sweetheart? Going to wait until the cavalry shows up? Because I've got bad news for you, Janey. This will all be over before they can even get here."

Where the small muscles in her face slackened, she noted all of the wonderful muscle in Sullivan's body went rock hard, even from this distance. His eyes widened. "Jane!"

Strong arms wrapped around her from behind, picking her up off her feet. Jane threw her head back, hitting solid bone, but whoever had her wasn't going to let a broken nose stop him. Sullivan lunged for her, but Christopher landed a hit to the gash in his side, and the SEAL went down. Sullivan's groan echoed all around her. She struggled inside the suffocating grip squeezing the oxygen from her body, her arms and legs fighting her brain's commands. Her vision blurred, and the gun fell from her hand.

"I'm a killer, Jane, and I've been doing this a long time now. I learn from my mistakes," Christopher said. Both mercenaries collected their weapons. Christopher planted a boot along Sullivan's spine, pressing his bare chest into the snow-covered ground, and widened his arms straight out to his sides. "You chose an ex–navy SEAL to protect you. I chose to bring a hell of a lot more men." He brushed the snow from his handgun and pressed a muddy boot into the side of Sullivan's head, taking aim. "And now, because of you, he's going to die."

"No!" Jane rocketed her elbow back into her attacker's stomach and then straight into his face when his grip lightened. She grabbed the fallen Glock at her feet and pumped her legs, the air in her lungs freezing. The mercenary at Christopher's side ran to head her off. The distance between them closed fast. She wasn't strong enough to take him alone, but Jane had run out of options. Sullivan wasn't going to die because of her. Not ever.

A sniper shot echoed from beyond the tree line, then ripped through the oncoming mercenary's collarbone. Jane watched as his face contorted into painful surprise and he dropped to his knees. In her next breath, he fell face-first into the snow, as another bullet took care of the contract killer rushing up behind her.

"Too late, Janey." Christopher squeezed the trigger. Sullivan's body jerked as the mercenary crouched low, desperation to survive bright in his dark eyes.

"Sullivan!" He'd been hit. Jane lunged. Her left shoulder slammed into Christopher, and she pushed as hard as she could to get him off his feet. The world spun as they rolled together through the snow. Once. Twice.

Christopher dug his fingernails into her arms, keeping her close, controlling her movements. She fought to dislodge the gun from his thigh holster, but couldn't get her arms free. He pinned her to the ground and smiled. He had her right where he wanted her, and her stomach revolted. "Just like old times, Janey. Remember?"

"Get your hands off her." Christopher's weight disappeared as Sullivan ripped him back. The mercenary stumbled but straightened fast. Blood dripped down Sullivan's side and from the bullet wound in his opposite shoulder. No normal man could survive that much damage and still have the strength to fight a contract killer.

But Sullivan Bishop was no ordinary man.

He swung, connecting with Christopher's face, his kidneys, his spine. The mercenary kept trying to block the hits, but Sullivan didn't let up, like a boxer who knew it'd be his last fight. Christopher wobbled on his feet, mouth hanging open, one eye swelling shut.

Jane stood, collecting her discarded Glock from the snow. Blood rushed to her head, but she stumbled after them as they neared the tree line. Those sniper shots that'd taken out Christopher's team said the Blackhawk Security team was close. If Sullivan knocked the mercenary out long enough to restrain him, Elliot or Anthony could haul him in while Jane got Sullivan to the hospital. His strength wouldn't last forever. Already, his punches weren't having the same effect, and Christopher realized it.

And then Christopher produced something in his hand. The mercenary ran forward, shoving a blade up and under Sullivan's rib cage.

"No!" She ran hard as Christopher dropped Sullivan to the ground. No. This wasn't happening. "Sullivan." Her senses sharpened. Jane was already raising the gun. Her finger was on the trigger as Christopher limped toward her, Sullivan's blood on his hands. And she fired, hitting the vulnerable flesh just below his Kevlar vest.

The mercenary froze in his tracks, mouth still open.

She fired again and again and again. Blistering cold worked to freeze the tears streaking down her cheeks, but Jane emptied the magazine until the gun merely clicked in her hand.

Christopher collapsed into the snow. Dead.

Her shoulders dropped. Rushing past his worthless body, she fell at Sullivan's side. He stared straight up into the sky. "No, no, no, no. Sullivan, come on. Stay with me."

"You did it, Jane." His voice strained, something wet and guttural choking his words.

"*We* did it. It's over." She'd pulled him through the Alaskan wilderness once. She could do it again to get him the help he desperately needed. "Come on. We need to get you inside before you freeze to death."

The trees to her left shifted, and Jane raised the gun. She'd emptied the magazine into Christopher. No time to go for Sullivan's stash of weapons in the cabin. Without any rounds left in the Glock, she couldn't stop more attackers in their tracks, but Christopher's men weren't taking her from Sullivan. She might be a lawyer, but she'd kill everyone who tried before leaving him to die here alone. Two figures burst from the tree line, both heavily armed, and Jane's arm sank with the weight of the gun. Elliot and Anthony rushed forward, the weapons expert already barking orders into the radio in his hand.

"Jane." Sullivan wrapped his fingers around hers, his pupils growing bigger until limited amounts of the sea blue she'd started falling in love with remained. Bringing the back of her hand to his mouth, he kissed the sensitive skin there and a chill swept through her. "Go."

"I'm not leaving you." Hot tears fell onto his chest, smudging lines of blood. "This is all my fault."

A soft thumping reverberated across the property, but Jane had attention for only the man who'd nearly died to save her life. The man she'd blackmailed into this. Her hair whipped in front of her face. Where had the wind come from?

"Jane, you need to get out of the way." Rough hands wrapped around her upper arms, but she shrugged them away. She wasn't sure who'd grabbed her. Didn't matter. "The EMTs have to get through."

"Help him." She held on to Sullivan's hand tighter. "Please, help him."

"Jane, come on." Elliot's voice filtered through the fog around her brain. He tugged her free of

Sullivan's grip as a team of EMTs closed in a tight circle around him. "You don't want to see this."

"This is all my fault. I'm sorry." Jane couldn't think. Couldn't breathe. Legs weak as Elliot dragged her against him and carried her away, Jane kept her eyes locked on Sullivan's motionless hand against the spreading red snow. "I'm so sorry."

# Chapter Twelve

Bullets. Blood. Scars. Some things never changed.

A groan vibrated through Sullivan's chest as he straightened in the hospital bed. Hell, that hurt. But the pain and haziness disappeared as he caught sight of a beautiful head of short black hair sprawled across the white sheets on one side of his bed.

Jane.

He sat forward, brushing a strand of soft hair away from her face. Her breathing sped up, and a smile pulled at one side of his mouth. He'd never get used to the way she reacted to him when he touched her. She'd wrapped her long fingers around his before falling asleep, and he didn't dare pull away. With her fast asleep, the nightmares of the last five days had slipped from her features. The bruise along her cheek had lightened, the cut across her head healing without stitches. Not an ounce of fear pulled her expression taut. She looked peaceful. For once. He'd traveled the world, experienced the most amazing and destructive forces of nature, but Jane Reise was by far the most amazing.

And his.

*This isn't over with me, you know. I'm not the only one he hired.* Menas. Sullivan tightened his grip around Jane's hand. The mercenary had deserved every bullet she'd emptied into him, but this was far from over. Whoever had hired Menas and his team wasn't finished. Not until Jane's heart stopped beating, which wouldn't happen. Because he'd take another hundred stabs to the torso by another dozen mercenaries if it meant she got to walk away from this. And she would. They both would.

"I don't think I've ever seen you smile at another human being like that. A piece of chocolate cake, yes. Not a woman." Anthony Harris's forest green eyes—free of sunglasses—locked on to Sullivan. The former Ranger buried his hands deep into his jacket pockets as though he didn't know what to do without a gun in his grip. Which was probably why he kept scanning the room for potential threats. Anthony cleared his throat. "If someone made me happy like that, I'd fight like hell to keep her with me, too."

The number one thing Sullivan could count

on his weapons expert for? The blatant truth, even when his trigger-happy best friend should keep his mouth shut. "How long has she been here?"

"She hasn't left your side since the EMTs brought you through the front doors. Wouldn't let the technicians look at her until they got your stats stable." Anthony rolled his wrist to check his watch. "Going on thirty hours. She's been asleep for about two."

Jane. Always putting others first, even when Menas had a gun aimed at her head.

Sullivan swallowed as the memories of the final battle with Menas flashed across his mind. He'd almost lost her. Again. But this time, it'd been his own fault. "Tell me how we missed the fact Christopher Menas was contracted to come after Jane."

"I've worked with guys like him and his team." Anthony shifted in his seat. "They've got the resources and the motives to create entire identities that hide what they do for a living. Some have two or three they cycle through to keep governments off their backs. Technically, they don't exist. No families. No friends. They're good at what they do. But Menas. Man, this guy is something else."

"He used his real name." Sullivan's gaze

flickered to the rise and fall of Jane's chest. Why would a mercenary take the chance of being identified? He rested his head back against the mountain of pillows behind him. "He wanted Jane to know he was coming after her."

*To throw off suspicion of the real threat?*

"How did Menas manage to escape your and Elliot's detail?" he asked.

"He knew we were there. He sent a four-man team straight at us as he and three others sped from the construction site." Spreading one hand over his beard, Anthony let his eyebrows hike higher, a telling sign of stress. "I tried calling, but you never answered your phone."

Because he'd tossed it to the floor to have a few more minutes with Jane. Damn it. This whole thing could've been avoided had he just been able to keep his hands off her. He'd put her in danger. He'd *failed* her. Sullivan studied the rise and fall of Jane's back. She'd gone up against a mercenary. To save his life. Again. Shaking the disbelief from his thoughts, he dropped the back of his head to the pillows propping him up. He could really fall for this woman. He ran his free hand down his face. Hell, maybe he already had.

"Call Elizabeth. I want a list of Menas's associates, his phone records from the cell you recovered from the cabin, his laptop if you can track it down, travel records and anything else she can get her hands on. Jane said the stalking started while she was on tour. Find out who else on our suspect list has made a visit to Afghanistan." Sullivan ripped the IV out of the catheter in his inner wrist. Stinging pain radiated up his arm, but he pushed it to the back of his mind. He'd survived worse. "Get it to me as soon as possible."

Anthony speed-dialed Blackhawk Security's resident former NSA analyst and shut the door behind him. They wouldn't have the intel for at least another hour. Enough time for Sullivan to put a new plan in place. With Menas's team out of commission, they were back at square one. But the question had changed from who was stalking Jane to who wanted her dead enough to hire a contract killer?

A soft moan whispered from between her lips, and Jane's hold on his hand tightened. He stroked his fingers along the inner line of her wrist, bringing her around slowly. She lifted her head, a smile pulling at the edges of her delicate mouth. Those hazel eyes brightened as she studied him. "You're awake." She pulled her hand from his and pressed her palms into her eye sockets. He'd never tire of the huskiness in her voice when she woke, an experience he intended to live over and over. She sat back in the chair, stretching her neck to one side, then the other. "How are you feeling?"

"I'll live. Thanks to you." He hadn't been okay with her stepping between him and Menas at the time, but without her rushing the mercenary at the last second, Sullivan would've died from high-speed lead poisoning. He owed her his life. Again. "How many times have you saved my life now? Two or three?"

"Three." A flash of straight white teeth deepened the laugh lines around her mouth and Sullivan's heart stuttered. "Should I make another reference to how the army comes in to save the day or let it be this time around?"

"I knew you were going to go there. You grunts never could take a win humbly. Got to let the whole world know you saved the day." He shook his head, but had never felt so relaxed, so…at peace than he did in that moment. Anthony had been right. Jane made him happy, gave him purpose beyond running Blackhawk Security, and a reason to look forward to the future. And he'd fight like hell to keep her.

"You always know what to say." Jane slid her hand back into his, a few cuts and bruises decorating the thin skin along the top of her hand. Her smile disappeared. Connecting that beautiful gaze with his, she rolled her bottom lip between her teeth. Not a good sign. "My leave is due to end in two days, Sullivan. The army was generous enough to give me these last few months off, but with the threat gone—" she inhaled slowly "—with Christopher gone, I need to get back to work. In Afghanistan."

The pad of his thumb stopped midstroke against the back of her hand. *Afghanistan?* "You're leaving."

Not a question. Sullivan rested his head back against the pillow, staring up at the ceiling. How could he have been so stupid? Of course she'd planned on going back to Afghanistan. Her life was there. Her job was there. At least, until she was reassigned.

"Unless…" she said.

He straightened. "Unless, what?"

"Unless I put in to be reassigned here in Anchorage." That gut-wrenching smile of hers returned, and Sullivan couldn't help but hang on every word. "There's an opening at Joint Base Elmendorf-Richardson, and I'm thinking of taking it. It'd be a step down in salary for me, but Anchorage could be my last assignment before I have the option of discharge in about a year.

My CO has already said the position's mine. All I have to do is ask."

"Then ask." The words were out of his mouth before he had a chance to think about what he was asking of her. He exhaled hard, but the tendons between his neck and shoulder strained. Sitting up as best he could, Sullivan ignored the pain shooting throughout his torso and brought Jane up onto the bed. Damn if he popped a few stitches. Jane was worth every ounce of agony. "I'm not going to lie. I'm not going to play games with you. I want you to ask for the transfer. I want you to stay here, with me."

Her heart beat fast against the soft column of her throat. He'd caught her off guard. Good. Smoothing her fingers over his arms, she studied him from the waist up. "Great. Because I already put the call in to my CO while you were passed out. He's sending me the papers in the morning."

Sullivan threaded his fingers through her hair and brought her mouth to his. He drank her in, memorized her in ways he'd never experienced before. He kept the kiss soft when all he wanted to do was claim her. She was staying. For him. For them. Tilting her head to the side, she opened her mouth wide, inviting him, nipping at him. She pressed herself against him, but the leads connected to strategic points on his body were determined to block his access to her. The EKG pounded loud in his ears, an echo of his own heart rate, and Sullivan couldn't drown the laugh rumbling through his chest. He gently framed her jaw with both hands, calluses against silk, and put a few small centimeters between them. "Any more of this and the nurses are going to run in here thinking I'm having a heart attack."

His hospital room door opened, but he couldn't focus on anything but her. His Jane.

"As much as I'd like to leave you two to go at it like rabbits," Anthony said, "I've got that new intel you wanted."

Sullivan's stomach sank. Right. The world wouldn't stop just for them. "Anything we can use?"

"New intel?" Jane studied Anthony, then turned back to him, eyebrows drawn inward. She checked the clock on the wall. "Oh. If this is another case, I can go. I'm supposed to give my statement to Anchorage PD in a few minutes anyway." She gathered her jacket in one hand and stood. "Then I need to go home and change."

Sullivan clamped his hand around her arm, staring up at her without any idea how he would tell her the truth. He owed her an answer, owed her far more than that, but his instincts screamed he was about to lose Jane all over again. Right when they'd agreed to give this a shot. But if she discovered the truth on her own? He'd never see her again. "It's not a new case, Jane." He licked his bottom lip, a nervous habit of hers he'd obviously inherited since setting sights on her in his office. "It's your case."

"What do you mean? Christopher is dead. My case is closed." Her eyes narrowed as seconds passed. Confusion slipped over her perfect features. "I shot him seven times, Sullivan. He's officially been declared dead."

"Christopher Menas was paid to take you out, Jane." He clamped his hand around hers, desperate to keep her within arm's reach. Not for her—Jane was strong—but for his own selfish need to hold on to her. "And whoever hired him is still after you."

"WHAT?" PANIC THREATENED to overwhelm her. No. The nightmare was over. She was supposed to get her life back. She'd put in for the transfer to Anchorage to start over. She and Sullivan were going to try to make this work. The room spun and Jane gripped the sheets for balance.

Someone had hired Menas to come after her? "Who...who would hire a mercenary team to take me out?"

She was one woman. A lawyer for the army with no record of sending innocent soldiers to their deaths, not someone with a highly politicized agenda. She mostly dealt with divorces, immigration and passport issues, and reenlistment questions when she wasn't assigned to prosecute cases. She wasn't important.

"That's what I'm trying to find out. Anthony has worked with men like Menas before. I'm hoping we can get a hit off a source in one of his circles. I also asked my NSA contact to pull phone records." Sullivan wrapped his strong, steady hand around hers. "Menas would've had contact with whoever hired him. We're going to find out how."

This wasn't happening.

Christopher was dead. Despite her initial intentions to bring him to justice, she'd *killed* him and almost lost Sullivan in the process. Her hands shook as she dropped her hold on the sheets and fisted a handful of her own hair instead. Thirty hours. That was all the relief she'd had with Christopher's death. What was she supposed to do now?

Slivers of blood seeped through Sullivan's bandages. A bullet wound, a knife to the gut and a slash across the arm. She couldn't remember how many stitches the doctor had told her they'd had to sew in to keep him together, but he couldn't go through that again.

"Jane, I need to know what's going through your head, baby." Sullivan rubbed small circles into the back of her hand. The weight of those captivating sea-blue eyes studying her was almost suffocating. "Tell me."

She couldn't go home. Couldn't go back to work. And she couldn't keep putting the man she'd started to fall for in harm's way. Not for her.

Whoever'd hired Christopher Menas and his team had done their research on her, and if Christopher was reporting back, they knew she'd recruited Sullivan to keep her safe. She exhaled hard. Sullivan had done his job. He'd found her stalker. Her muscles tightened. Now she had to learn to protect herself. Jane stood, slipping out of his grasp a little too easily. He'd let her go. Because that was the kind of man he was. Considerate. Caring. Never one to thwart her own agency. She headed for the door. "I have to go."

"For how long?" he asked.

The rough edge to his tone revealed exactly what she'd feared, and Jane stopped cold. He'd either read her mind or read her expression, she didn't know. It didn't matter. She had to get out of here. Away from him. Away from the whole Blackhawk Security team. The nightmare wasn't ever going to end. They were all still in danger as long as she stuck around. Anthony waited in front of the door, capable of keeping her here if Sullivan ordered. But he wouldn't. She had to believe that.

"Jane, we can fight this thing together. You don't have to run." His voice washed over her in comforting waves, and it took everything she had not to turn back around. "Please. I don't want to lose you."

"Then you know exactly how I feel." Jane turned, her heart overriding every logical thought speeding through her mind. She should've kept on walking, should've shoved Anthony out of the way and left this all behind. But she couldn't end things with Sullivan like this. Not after everything they'd been through. Five days, that was all it'd taken for her to fall for him. How was that possible? "Do you know how hard it was for me to watch you bleed out after Christopher was finished with you?"

She fought back the memories, her throat closing.

Sullivan straightened in the bed. "I can imagine."

"Those were the worst two minutes of my life, Sullivan." She hugged her jacket into her middle when all she really wanted to hold on to was lying in a hospital bed only a few feet away. "I warned you what happens to people who get close to me. And look where you are. Look at your body." She motioned to the darkening bandages taped all over his chest and shoulder. "But how is it going to end the next time? Or the time after that? I care about you, about what you want and need, and this isn't it."

"Jane, I can—"

"Take care of yourself," she finished for him. "I know. But you did your job. Christopher is dead. Now it's time for me to take care of myself." Jane headed toward the door, her insides twisting harder than ever before.

Sullivan hissed behind her, the machines he'd been hooked up to going haywire.

The look on Anthony's face as he lunged for the hospital bed spun her around. Ripping out the catheter and leads, Sullivan fought to stand beside the bed. His weapons expert offered a hand, but the stubborn SEAL brushed him off.

Her eyes widened, but Jane couldn't close the space between them. She'd fought too hard to get even this far. "Sullivan, what are you doing? You're going to rip your stitches out."

"Then I'll rip them out. I'm not letting you do this alone." He used the bed for support and shuffled forward. The hospital gown molded to him, a little too tight and too short for his musculature. "If that means we need to leave now, then we leave now. Anthony, go get the SUV. We'll meet you at the front."

"No. You're not going anywhere." The constant beeping from the machines would call the nurses and doctors in here in a few seconds, but even with their medical orders, Sullivan wouldn't stop until the job was done. Wasn't in his nature. She had to admire him for that, given that was exactly why she'd blackmailed him in the first place, but this time, Jane wouldn't stand by helpless when whoever hunted her caught up. And she wouldn't let Sullivan risk his life for her again, even if she had to go to extremes to stop him. "Do you remember what I said back in your office when you refused to help me?"

Fire consumed his gaze, almost hotter and wilder than when he'd taken on Christopher at the cabin. He fought to stand on his own, leaning against the bed rails, but Sullivan had lost a lot of blood. He wouldn't get far. "You wouldn't."

Jane stepped backward toward the door.

"Jane…" He pushed off from the bed, the muscles in his jawline ticking away with his erratic heartbeat. "Don't do this."

"You did your job, Sullivan. This is the only way to keep you safe. I'm sorry." She ripped open the door and shouted down the hall. "Police!"

Two uniformed Anchorage PD officers spun toward her from the end of the hall. She'd known they'd be there, waiting for her to give her statement. Both sprinted toward the room, hands on the butt of their guns, and hurried inside. "Ma'am?"

"This man isn't who he says he is. His real name is Sebastian Warren." Jane maneuvered closer to the door as they came inside the room, dread pooling at the base of her spine. This was the only way. "There's a warrant out for his arrest for murdering his father, the Anchorage Lumberjack, nineteen years ago."

The officers moved in, but Anthony constructed a barrier of hardened muscle before Sullivan set a tense hand on his weapon expert's shoulder and pushed him back. Fluorescent lighting glinted off a pair of handcuffs as the officers moved Sullivan back into the bed, but the SEAL only had attention for her.

The fire in his eyes had simmered, the remaining ashes full of…heartbreak?

A tight knot of hesitation spread through her, but Jane shoved her arms into her jacket as the officers started questioning Sullivan, and she slipped out the door. The cell phone she'd stolen from one of the officers was in her hand, her eye on the exit. She fought back the tears blurring her vision as she dialed the number she'd memorized for circumstances like this a few months ago. Never could be too careful. Off the grid. Leave everything behind.

"Jane!" Sullivan's voice echoed down the hallway, but she wouldn't turn back.

She unburied her own phone from her jacket pocket and tossed it into the garbage can against the wall. First thing Sullivan would do after posting bail would be to track her through her phone. He wanted to help, but she wouldn't lose him. Not the man who'd given her a reason to fight.

Keep moving. Don't look back. Bringing the stolen phone to her ear, she counted off the rings on the other line. Two. Three. The line picked up.

"Hey, it's me." Jane checked over her shoulder to make sure Sullivan hadn't ordered Anthony to follow her. Two nurses bolted into his room behind the Anchorage police officers as he shouted her name over and over again. She clutched the keys she'd taken off Anthony as he'd rushed to help Sullivan stand and focused on the double glass doors leading to the parking garage. Tears welled in her lower lash line, but Jane pushed them back. Turning him in might solidify her reputation, but her leaving ensured the safety of the one man she couldn't bear to lose. Sullivan. He was all that mattered now. "I need your help."

# Chapter Thirteen

"How didn't we see this coming?" Sullivan threw all of the team's research into a file box and shoved it across his desk. Pain shot up into his shoulder and across his rib cage as the box hit the floor and scattered the files from Jane's case across his office. The phone rang for the hundredth time in the last hour since he'd been released from Anchorage PD custody, intensifying the headache at the base of his skull. He pointed a finger at Elliot with the hand not strapped into a sling. "You're the private investigator. You're the one who should've been able to uncover Christopher Menas's true motive before this all blew up in our face."

"The guy was good at his job, Sullivan. I don't know what else you want me to say." Elliot collapsed back in one of the many leather chairs positioned in front of the CEO's massive oak desk, cell phone in hand. The brightness of the screen highlighted the stitches in his forehead from the fire at Menas's apartment, and regret flooded through Sullivan. In reality, they were lucky Elliot hadn't been killed, considering what Menas did for a living. "Besides, I think we all learned something very valuable here. Never trust the system. Everything you need to know is in a person's routines and daily life. Had we surveilled Menas before he'd tried killing us, I could've told you everything you'd needed to know."

"Who screwed up their job the most doesn't matter right now." Elizabeth Dawson, Blackhawk Security's head of network security, tossed a handful of manila file folders onto the gleaming desk between them. "We've got a client on the run, one who's probably scared out of her mind, and we have no idea who is after her. I'd say that qualifies as our first priority." The former NSA analyst nodded toward the pile of research. "Here's everything I could get my hands on for Christopher Menas. Phone records, emails, instant messages, bank accounts, payroll for his team, surveillance photos of Jane. I had to pull a few strings, so you owe me."

Every muscle in Sullivan's body tensed at the sound of her name. Damn it. Now wasn't the time to let emotion rule. His wrist still chafed where the Anchorage PD had cuffed him while they questioned him in that hospital bed for over twenty hours. The only reasons he'd been released after Jane's attempt to keep him off her case were a heavily funded bank account and the high-priced lawyer Blackhawk Security kept on retainer. But the nightmare wasn't over.

He'd killed his father before the psychopath could hurt anyone else. Sullivan had known this day would come. He locked his jaw. But, despite the possibility of spending the rest of his life in prison, he had more important things on his mind. First things first: find Jane. If he could talk to her—

"None of it tells me who might've hired Menas." Elizabeth leveraged her weight onto her hand against the desk, wide brown eyes only giving a hint of the off-the-charts intelligence behind them. "Either Christopher Menas was lying when he told you he'd been contracted to take Jane out, or the guy behind the curtain is one of the best shadow agents I've ever come across. And trust me, I know a few."

"He wasn't lying." Sullivan straightened. Head in the game. Get Jane to safety. "The entire reason he'd used his own name was to throw us off the scent of the real threat. Any word from Anthony?"

"Jane hasn't gone back to the town house, and there's no report from her CO either." Elliot held up his phone, waving it from side to side. "I went back through her bank records. No activity on her credit or debit cards, no withdrawals from her account. She has to be getting some kind of help to stay off the grid this long. As of right now, she's gone."

"Not acceptable." He'd never lost a mission or a client in all his time on this earth, and he wasn't about to start now. "We're just going to have to find the threat responsible for the price on Jane's head—" Sullivan ground his back molars, her name still sweet on his tongue "—before he finds her."

"This woman turned you over to the police and endangered the entire company. She doesn't want you on the case anymore, Sullivan." Vincent Kalani turned around from the other side of the office, uncrossing his arms. The forensics expert hadn't said another word this entire meeting, keeping to himself in the corner, but Sullivan read the resistance across his dark features. Shadows crossed Vincent's stern expression. Of all the men and women Sullivan had hired to create the Blackhawk Security team, Vincent had the uncanny ability to bring him back to earth when he was in over his head.

But not this time. "Are you going to put yourself—put *us*—back in this guy's crosshairs to save someone who doesn't want our help and who sold you out?"

"Yes." Because a man never gave up on the woman he loved. Sullivan ignored the burn of pain down his side. He inhaled deep, hoping to catch her vanilla scent in the air, but disappointment gripped him. Jane was running from whoever'd hired Menas, but also from him. She didn't want him in a position that would get him killed, but she didn't understand. He'd been in that position his entire life. First with his father, then the SEALs, now as part of the foremost private security consultancy in the United States. All of those moments had forged him into the man he was now, the man who could save her life. She'd just finally made the risk worth it.

"I built this company—and hired every single one of you—to save lives, and that's exactly what we're going to do. Save a life. Doesn't matter if we trust our clients. Doesn't matter if we like them. We have a responsibility to the people who walk through those doors, and today I only have attention for one of them. Jane Reise." Sullivan shifted his attention to Vincent. "But if you won't do the job I hired you for—" he nodded toward the double glass doors on the other side of his office "—there's the door. I don't have the time to question whether I can rely on you right now."

The phone rang again, attempting to break the tense silence descending between him and his team. Sullivan picked up the receiver and slammed it back down. He didn't have time for distractions either.

"Well, you got my vote, boss." Elliot stood, slapping his hand into Sullivan's. "But mostly because I'm terrified you're going to send me back to the prison you found me in if I don't comply."

A laugh rumbled through Sullivan's chest. "Don't you forget it, con man."

Elizabeth collected the files he'd tossed onto the floor and reorganized them across the desk. "I'll start combing through possible suspects in Jane's life again, targeting military personnel. Do you want me to call in Kate for another profile?"

"No. We can handle this without her." Blackhawk Security's profiler deserved all the time she could get after losing her husband to a random shooting two months ago. Sullivan wouldn't ask her to come back until she was ready. He ran over Elizabeth's words a second time. "Why target military personnel?"

"Someone this good at hiding his identity is a professional. At first I thought whoever hired Christopher Menas might've been former NSA, maybe current, but that doesn't add up. You said Jane was stalked in Afghanistan. The NSA hasn't had any assets there in over a year." Elizabeth brushed a piece of short brown hair behind her ear. Not quite as short as Jane's, but it accentuated her heart-shaped face and warm brown eyes, where Jane's gave the angles of her face more of an edge. "Without contacts within the intelligence community, our target wouldn't have been able to hire a mercenary team. On top of that, he knows her, he knows every detail of her life and has been following her across the globe. She doesn't have any relatives she's close to, so I've narrowed it down to three possibilities." Elizabeth ticked them off on her fingers one by one. "Our suspect is either her commanding officer, another lawyer who's worked with her or a criminal who's been prosecuted by her. All military."

"That's still a giant suspect pool, and Jane swore her CO didn't have anything to do with this when we first brought him up." Sullivan swiped his uninjured hand across his face, then focused on the hundreds of photos of Jane staring up at him from his desk. She'd disappeared twenty-four hours ago. She could be anywhere in the world. And so could her stalker. Hell. Sullivan curled his fingers into his palms, needing the small bite of pain to keep him focused. They didn't have time to make any more mistakes. "It'll take us weeks to sort through them all."

"I'll take her commanding officer." Vincent stepped close to the desk and motioned for Elizabeth to give him the file. The tribal tattoos climbing up his neck and down his arms stretched with the action. "He'd know her routine, her close friends in the JAG Corps and which defendants might want to take revenge. It's as good a place to start as any." He lifted his toffee-colored gaze to Sullivan.

"Thank you." Didn't matter that Jane had sworn up and down her CO had nothing to do with this. They'd run out of leads. Slapping his hand across Vincent's back, maybe a little too hard, he nodded. He rounded the desk and picked up one of the many photos Elliot had recovered from Christopher Menas's apartment before it'd been burned to the ground. "Now that only leaves about fifty more people we need to dig into, and any one of them could already be three steps ahead."

He didn't like those odds.

Sullivan studied the photo in his hand, his eyebrows drawing inward. It was a photo of Jane in court. Her hair was a little longer, nearly brushing her fatigues emblazoned with the JAG Corps insignia pinned to her chest. The walls were simple, bare, only two flags standing tall on either side of the judge. The American flag and the US Army flag. No other American insignia on the walls, which meant it probably wasn't an American courtroom. Could've been Afghanistan. There was no way to tell for sure, but Christopher Menas hadn't taken the picture. Jane would've recognized him in a heartbeat if her ex-college-boyfriend-turned-mercenary had sat a few feet from her.

"Boss?" Elliot asked. "Everything okay?"

From the angle of the photo, the picture had to have been taken by the defense's side of the courtroom. But why would a defendant or an attorney snap a picture in the middle of court, and where had Menas gotten the picture in the first place? Jane stood near the witness stand, not looking at the person who'd taken the photo. A surveillance photo. His stomach sank, but Sullivan rotated the photo in order to get a good look at the papers sprawled across the desk, any evidence that could point them in the right direction. A name. An official charge. A rank.

Something else caught his eye.

He brought the photo closer. The pen on the desk. Dread pooled at the base of his spine. He'd seen it before. But...

His cell phone chimed, and he read the incoming message from Anthony.

Subject has returned home.

He put the screen to sleep and shoved the phone into his pants pocket.

"I know who hired Christopher Menas." Sullivan snapped his head up. It didn't make sense, but he wasn't about to second-guess his instincts. Setting Jane's photo back onto the desk, he pulled his top desk drawer open and shoved his favorite Glock into his shoulder holster. There wasn't any time left. They had to get to Jane's town house now. "And I know why he's doing this."

CHRISTOPHER MENAS HAD gotten exactly what he'd wanted.

Captain Jane Reise of the United States JAG Corps no longer existed.

She stared down at the new passport, birth

certificate, driver's license and Social Security card on her lap, not sure why she hadn't gotten out of the car yet. The photos had been taken from her old passport, but the name, date of birth and address beside it had transformed her into someone completely different, thanks to a friend in the FBI's witness protection program. Sliding the airline ticket out from behind the thin leather, she memorized the information all over again. Her flight out of Ted Stevens International Airport to LAX left in two hours. Enough time to collect the cash she'd stashed beneath the floorboards under the right side of her bed. She couldn't use the money in her accounts. Too easy to trace. With that money, she'd have a fresh start. And there'd be no trace of her old life to follow.

The dropping temperatures were showing her breath, but Jane sat there, surveying the street for the hundredth time. No sign of an intruder, of a mercenary waiting for her to open the door. No sign of another Blackhawk Security vehicle either. Jane exhaled hard as pressure built behind her sternum. Sullivan hadn't come after her.

She pulled back her shoulders. She recalled the details of her new life. Now she was Rita Miller, a criminal defense lawyer from Los Angeles, California, who worked for a large firm right in the center of the city. She had no idea how her friend in the FBI had managed to pull that off, but did it matter?

She craned her head over her shoulder toward the town house again. So, in reality, the rental wasn't even hers anymore. All of the furniture, her clothing, the small possessions she'd collected from her travels over the last few years would be sold off in some estate sale. Her father and his new family wouldn't want them and Jane wasn't allowed to pack and ship them to her new address in California, according to the rules. Leave everything behind. Leave *everyone* behind.

The rules. A small burst of laughter had her setting the crown of her head against the headrest. Frayed wiring dangled from the control panel centered above the rearview mirror. Sullivan really should've been more careful about concealing the tracking devices he'd installed in his vehicles. Or at least have a backup. Staring up at the SUV's ceiling, she closed her eyes. She'd worked her entire life sticking to the rules, bending them to fit her or her clients' needs, but never breaking them, and she'd done a good job.

Until five days ago.

She'd broken the first rule she'd given herself when breaking into Sullivan Bishop's office: don't fall in love. And look where breaking the rules had landed her. Sitting outside her own town house in the middle of the night in freezing temperatures because she couldn't bear the thought of what she might find inside.

Or who.

Her lower lash line burned. She swiped at the runaway tear streaking down her face. This was stupid. Sullivan hadn't followed her. He wasn't waiting inside for her to come home. Jane dropped her chin to her chest, opening her eyes. "Screw the rules."

This was the only way to start over, to save the man she'd blackmailed into protecting her.

She tossed the new passport into the passenger-side seat and jammed her shoulder into the door of the Blackhawk Security SUV she'd borrowed from the hospital garage. She'd take the SUV to the airport, then let Elliot or Anthony know where they could pick it up. There was a good chance she'd change her mind if she talked to Sullivan again. Although, with how she'd left things between them in the hospital, him in handcuffs, her running out the door, he might make it easier than she imagined.

Jane jogged across the street, keeping an

eye out for any movement, any glare of head-lights coming to life. The key was already in her hand, in case she had to get inside in a hurry. She twisted the key in the lock and pushed the door inward. A wall of hot air rushed against her, relieving some of the tightness in her lower back. She tossed her keys onto the table by the door, as she did every day, and closed the door behind her, locking it. Her throat went dry. It still smelled like him. Her attention shot to the makeshift bed on the couch where Sullivan had slept, and she shuffled toward it. Slumping down onto the couch, she stared at what remained of the space she used to consider a safe haven.

The town house had been tossed. Clothing, books, photos, all destroyed. She couldn't imagine how many people had trudged through her personal belongings, picked apart her life since she'd run off into the middle of the night after a murderer. Police, Sullivan's team, Christopher Menas. But, here, surrounded by the scent of the man she'd unwillingly surrendered to, her muscles slowly released. It was over. For now. The man who'd turned her life upside down for the past couple of months—who'd tried to kill her was dead. Of course, someone had hired Christopher's band of mercenaries in the first place, but she couldn't think about that right now. A few more minutes of relief was all she needed. Then she'd get the cash and lock up for good. No looking back. A fresh start.

There should've been some relief in that thought, but all Jane could think about was the look on Sullivan's face when she'd called for the police. Christopher Menas would've killed her had it not been for Sullivan. And she'd thrown it in his face. She'd hurt him—badly—and she wasn't sure if there was any way he'd trust another woman again. Or forgive her.

She rubbed her fingers into her sternum to counteract the pain spreading through her chest. Sullivan had forgiven her for her part in Marrok's suicide, but he had every reason to hate her now. Tears welled in her eyes again, but Jane wiped them away.

She couldn't believe what she was about to do.

She was going to find Sullivan. Witness protection could wait. She had to fix this. No matter how long it took or how many times he slammed the door in her face, she'd make this right.

Because she couldn't imagine another day of her life without Sullivan Bishop—or Sebastian Warren—in it. She loved him. Threading the sheets between her fingers, Jane relaxed back against the couch. She loved him. Why had it taken her so long to realize it? She was an idiot. Of course she'd fallen for him. Sullivan protected people for a living, protected her. He stood against the evil in this world and smiled while doing it. He'd committed himself one hundred percent to the job and refused to stop when the chances of dying skyrocketed. But the best part? The way he'd looked at her while he did it, like he could've loved her back. The way he held her, ready to take a bullet to keep her safe... Jane thunked her head against the back of the couch. And wasn't that a kick to the stomach? She ground her back molars.

She'd made a mistake.

Hefting herself from the couch coated in Sullivan's clean, masculine scent, she stepped over the debris toward her bedroom. The damage extended up the stairs and through to the main bathroom, but Jane didn't have the energy to start cleaning. Wasn't any point now. After she saw Sullivan, she wasn't coming back. Every muscle in her body ached. Take a shower. Call the hospital, the police department, Blackhawk Security, whoever she had to call to track Sullivan down. In that order. She discarded her jacket onto the ottoman at the foot of her bed and turned. She hit a wall of solid muscle.

"Tell me, Captain Reise, does this rag smell like chloroform to you?" a voice from the past asked. A hand clamped a white rag over her mouth as another grabbed the back of her head to keep her in place against his chest. "Shh. It'll all be over soon."

Jane threaded her hands between his arms and looped them wide. The cloth over her mouth disappeared, but an acrid taste spread across her tongue as she lunged for the bedroom door. Her fight-or-flight response kicked into high gear. This wasn't possible. Searing pain spread over her skull as he fisted a handful of her hair and pulled her back into him. Her fingers automatically shot to her head to relieve the pain, and he clamped the soaked rag over her mouth again.

Jane kicked and kneed at him, grabbing onto his wrists to dislodge his hold. But he was strong. Too strong. And she'd lost too much energy over the last few days. She couldn't control her breathing, the poison working down into her system too fast for her to keep up the fight. The edges of her vision darkened. *No. Stay awake. Leave evidence.* Sullivan had to know...

Her grip lightened, her muscles protesting

the orders her brain gave. Jane wrapped her left hand around the closest thing she could grab from her attacker's button-down shirt pocket. A single pen. Her legs gave out.

"That's it." He led her to the floor but refused to remove the rag from her mouth. "Just relax. You're in good hands."

Her arm arched up above her head, and she let the pen slip from her hold. It rolled under the bed. Staring up into the face of her attacker, Jane couldn't move, couldn't keep her eyes open as the darkness closed in. The shadows across his sharp, angled jawline shifted as he pressed her into the floor. She'd recognize that face anywhere. Her eyebrows drew inward as she squinted away the blurriness closing in. "Not... you."

"That's right, Jane. Me." He bent low over her, the scars across his eyebrows and chin deeper than she remembered. His breath snaked across the underside of her neck. She tried to pull away, tried to run, but couldn't stay awake. Her eyelids sagged closed. "And now it's my turn to torture *you*."

# Chapter Fourteen

Sullivan clutched the only piece of evidence he and his team had recovered from Jane's town house as he sped down the highway: the pen. It'd rolled under her bed, but his instincts screamed that Jane had been trying to leave him a clue as to who'd taken her.

And there was only one place her stalker would hide to get his attention. The cabin.

"I'm coming, Jane. I'm coming." He'd promised to keep her safe, and he intended to keep every promise he'd made to her. Murky water kicked up along the SUV's windows as he pressed his foot harder against the pedal. The wipers crossed the windshield in the same rhythm his heart tried to beat out of his chest. This whole thing hadn't been about Jane, at least not entirely. His past had come back to haunt him, too. He just didn't have all the pieces yet. Sullivan rotated the wheel to the left, taking the SUV down the snow-coated trail. Pain zinged through his arm and side, but he only gripped the steering wheel tighter.

Clouds and short bursts of wind dumped flakes onto the windshield. The closer he got to his destination, the less he could see, nearly everything in sight a complete whiteout. Rubbing the inside of the windshield clear of fog, Sullivan squinted through the snow. He should be coming up on the cabin any second now—

A black blur appeared directly in the SUV's path.

"Damn it!" He spun the SUV to the left, straight into the tree line, and slammed on the brakes. Adrenaline flooded into his veins, heart rate rocketing. The back end of the GMC fishtailed, and time seemed to slow. Sullivan turned into the spin, breath frozen in his throat. He fought to keep control of the vehicle. The back end of the SUV missed an unconscious Jane by mere inches, but he couldn't correct in time.

The GMC slammed into a thick tree, and he hit the steering wheel hard. A cascade of snow fell over the crumpled hood as the engine died. Shoving himself back in his seat, he brushed his fingertips across his forehead. Blood dripped down the side of his face. It was a miracle he hadn't lost consciousness. His breath sawed in and out of his lungs, but he clamped on to the door handle. "Jane."

Shoving his recently stitched shoulder into the door, Sullivan suppressed a scream as agony washed over him. He tumbled out of the SUV. His boots slid along the compacted snow, and he collapsed against the GMC. The pain dissipated, slowly, but he had to push it to the back of his mind. *Get to Jane. Neutralize the threat.* He kept his breathing shallow, even, and opened his eyes.

Hands tied behind the back of a chair, Jane sat slumped over her legs, unconscious, about twenty feet away. She hadn't realized he'd almost killed her coming to save her life. Relief, however fleeting, flooded through him, and he took the magazine out of his Glock and shoved it back into place. But he didn't make a move toward her. Nobody put a victim in the middle of the road like that unless they intended to take the high ground to watch the chaos unfold. Dread coiled a tight fist in the pit of his stomach. There was only one way this could end. Her kidnapper wanted a show? Sullivan would give him one.

"I know you're out there," he shouted over his shoulder. Sullivan pressed his back into the SUV for cover, finger on the trigger. His head throbbed, heart beating loudly, but the soft crunching of snow reached his ears. His target froze in his tracks, approximately ten yards to the southeast, just on the other side of the road. "Let's finish this."

Sullivan bounded away from the SUV and swung his gun up and around.

And froze.

"Hey, big brother." Acrid smoke filled the air around Marrok Warren. He tossed the lit cigar into the snow and stomped it out with his boot, the butt of a gun peeking out from under his jacket. Thick brown hair covered the scars Sullivan had witnessed cut into his younger brother's chin by their father when they'd been younger. Deep lines wrinkled the top of Marrok's forehead as he unholstered the weapon at his side. "Guess you never expected to see me again."

"Not after I buried you next to Mom. No, I did not." His recovery of the pen their mother had given Marrok when he'd turned twelve had told Sullivan exactly what—*who*—to expect on the wrong end of his gun, but Sullivan swallowed hard. He shifted his stance wide and readjusted his grip on the Glock. "You faked your death in order to torture Jane for prosecuting you."

"What's a little revenge among friends? I certainly had a good time terrorizing her the past three months. Then she hired you, and I had to up the stakes. Playtime was over." Marrok circled to his right, putting him in the center of the road. "Sebastian Warren. My big brother. Always the *savior*. Always the hero."

"So now you're blaming me for keeping you alive for all those years Dad came after you?" A burst of laughter exploded from between Sullivan's teeth. He shook his head, gun still aimed as he counteracted his brother's movements. "You're sick, Marrok. I can get you help."

"Thanks for the offer, big brother, but I wouldn't be the man I am now had it not been for Dad's influence. If I hadn't followed in his footsteps, I wouldn't have the connections or the money I do now. And, let me tell you, it was all worth it. Only difference between Dad and me? My tastes are a little more…" Marrok's dark eyes flickered past Sullivan. To Jane. One scarred edge of his mouth turned upward. "Refined."

The muscles surrounding his spine hardened one by one. Sullivan had buried his brother as a hero, put him to rest next to their mother in their hometown cemetery. He'd believed in his innocence for over a year. "Jane was right about you all along. You assaulted those women while you were on tour."

Marrok drove his hand into his jacket pocket, extracting a small black device. "You can't win this fight, Sebastian. Don't forget, I know you better than anyone else. You're just using a different name now." His younger brother wiggled the device for Sullivan to see, then raised his gun and took aim. At Sullivan's heart. "I know you won't kill me because you can't stand the thought of killing your own brother, but I also know you'd do anything to save an innocent life. Especially one you've been taking to bed."

"I know you, too, little brother. You're not going to shoot me." Sullivan fought to relieve the searing pain spreading down his side. Marrok had been watching them this whole time? A sick feeling rolled through him. His brother was right. He wouldn't kill Marrok, but that didn't mean he couldn't make him pay for what he'd done. He tightened his grip around the gun as he backed up a few feet to where Jane sat. Sullivan tipped her head back and his stomach sank. Pressing his fingers to her throat, he counted off the slow, uneven rhythm in his head. Her lips had turned blue, the blistering cold slowing down her heart rate, but the bomb vest strapped to her chest kicked his up a notch.

"No, Sebastian. You *knew* me. Then you abandoned me for the navy, leaving me behind to deal with the aftermath you caused after killing Dear-Old-Dad, and never looked back. Even changed your name so I couldn't track you down. Now I find you're protecting the one person I hate most in the world. *Jane Reise*." Her sweet name growled from between Marrok's lips as he nodded toward Jane. "So you're right. I might not put a bullet in you, but I sure as hell won't feel guilty if you're caught in the crossfire."

"Marrok." Sullivan took a single step forward, his ears going numb from the pounding wind. "Everything I did, I did for you, to protect—"

"You can save the speech, big brother. I know the truth. You've always wanted to escape the life we had, and killing our father gave you a way to do it." Marrok held up the device in his hand, pointing it toward Jane. "You're a SEAL. You know what this is and what will happen if you're anywhere close to her when that bomb blows."

"Jane, baby." No answer. He brushed her hair back from her face, then straightened. "Can you hear me?"

"You don't get a choice in this, Sebastian,

and you're running out of time." Keeping the gun aimed at Sullivan's chest, Marrok walked backward down the road slowly. "It's over. She gets what she deserves and we all move on with our lives."

"No." The growl reverberated through him. Move on without Jane? A small burst of wind dislodged the piles of snow lining the tree branches, whiting out visibility between them, and Sullivan had his shot.

"Jane *is* my life." He sprinted with every bit of energy his battered body could produce, the icy air filling his lungs. But the wind died too fast, and he found himself out in the open. Still, Sullivan didn't slow.

Eyes wide, Marrok squeezed off one round, which went wide. Then another, hitting Sullivan in the right arm. A third round lodged in his upper thigh. He didn't care. Blood dripped down his fingers, but he wouldn't stop. Because he loved Jane. Didn't matter when it'd happened. Didn't matter how. All that mattered was that it'd happened. He'd fallen in love with the one woman he'd vowed to condemn for the rest of his life.

Sullivan's jaw strained against his body's screams for relief. But without that detonation device, he'd lose everything. He rammed his shoulder under Marrok's ribs, tackling his brother to the ground. He pulled back his elbow, only the slightest hesitation gripping him. Enough time for Marrok to take advantage.

"You shouldn't have gotten involved, big brother." Marrok slammed the butt of his gun into Sullivan's head.

Scalding pain spread over his skull as Marrok kicked him backward. Sullivan hit the ground, cushioned by two feet of snow. Memories of countless nights, of holding a baseball bat or a knife or a gun in the back of their shared closet to protect his younger brother, flashed across his mind. He'd done what he'd had to, to protect his family. But the one person he'd never counted on turning on him had lost his damn mind. His gaze shot to Jane as her head fell to one side. She was coming around. And she needed him to protect her now.

"You were right, though. I don't like the idea of killing you either. There's a reason Menas drugged and Tasered you first." Marrok shifted his finger over the trigger of his gun. "But I will end you now if you choose Jane Reise over your own flesh and blood."

Sullivan pushed to his feet and maneuvered into the middle of the road, right between Marrok and Jane. The gun was pointed straight at him. A blast of wind kicked up snow as it swept across the clearing beside his cabin. His right arm and thigh burned from the two rounds Marrok had squeezed off. No major damage, but enough to pull at his attention. He was a SEAL, hardened and trained in every kind of environment. He didn't need to see the threat to neutralize it. A glint of sunlight off glass caught his attention from the tree line, and a smile pulled at one side of his mouth. "If you know me so well, then you know I don't stop until the job is done. And we're not done."

"I thought you might say something like that." Marrok shrugged, gun in one hand, the detonator in the other. With one click of a button, his younger brother would take everything from him. "Just like I know you brought your team to take me out in case things went south."

Marrok's gaze flickered over his shoulder as Anthony and Elliot burst through the trees, each armed and ready to neutralize the threat on Sullivan's orders. "Well, guess what, big brother? Things are about to go south." Raising the gun to Sullivan's head, Marrok compressed the detonator. "I'll see you in hell, Sebastian."

"No!" Sullivan lunged, focused solely on the detonator and not the gun aimed between his eyes.

As Marrok pulled the trigger.

THE GUNSHOTS HAD brought her around. All too familiar.

"Sullivan." His name barely whispered from her lips, her body fighting her brain's commands. Jane struggled against the rope at her wrists and ankles, but couldn't move. The brightness of the snow blinded her. Had Marrok Warren finally killed her?

She had to warn Sullivan.

Her eyelids were heavy, but Jane managed to roll her head to one side. Either hell had frozen over or she was actually strapped to a chair in the middle of the Alaskan wilderness. What had Marrok planned for her? Leave her to the wolves? Not very original.

Catching sight of two dark gray rocks half-buried in the snow beside her, she curled her fingers into her palms. She couldn't move. Couldn't scream from the effects of the chloroform. Couldn't protect herself. But she'd be damned if she didn't go down fighting like Sullivan had taught her.

*Get out of the chair. Get to Sullivan.* She twisted hard, tipping the chair into the snow. Air crushed from her lungs as she sent flakes above her head. Her fingers brushed against the rough edges of one rock and she stretched her hands as far as they would go to grab it. The ties were too tight, and her body was so tired. Marrok would get what he wanted, and Sullivan... No. She couldn't think about that. Her fingertips brushed against the rough surface of one rock. *There.*

Relief flooded through her as she grabbed the rock and hacked away at the rope. The ties fell from around her wrists, and she maneuvered out from under the chair. Bending to cut through the rope at her ankles, Jane caught a flash of red across her abdomen and, for a moment, she assumed it was blood. But the color was off. Brighter. And the flash disappeared, then reappeared. She squinted at the message glowing from the display, her mouth going dry. *Armed.* More colors claimed her attention. These ones long and thin. Red, blue, green and white. Wires. Oxygen rushed from her lungs as she hastily cut through the rope at her feet.

Marrok had strapped her into a bomb vest? Running her and Sullivan off the road, trying to burn them to ashes in Menas's apartment and sending a mercenary detail after her in the first place hadn't been enough. He had to blow her up, too? All because she'd done her job.

Jane clawed at the vest but couldn't find a zipper or Velcro or anything to get her out of it. A guttural groan reached her ears and she spun toward the sound. Sullivan landed backward in the snow, and the man standing over him… "Marrok."

She didn't have a weapon—unless she counted the new piece of apparel strapped across her chest—but ran toward the fight anyway. The cold had drained energy from her muscles, but she pushed on even as Anthony and Elliot burst through the tree line and surrounded the man behind all of this. Sullivan shoved to his feet, and she nearly collapsed before leveraging her weight onto a nearby tree trunk. Shoving her hair out of her eyes, she breathed a little easier. He was okay. Marrok couldn't escape now. The army would take custody of him, and this whole thing would be over. She'd have her life back. She could go back to being Jane Reise.

But in the blink of an eye, Marrok Warren raised the gun to Sullivan's head. The world stopped spinning. Her hands tightened, her insides churned. No. This wasn't how this was supposed to end. Not him. Not because of her. Jane stumbled forward, closing the vast distance between them as fast as she could. Every cell in her body fought against the desperation clawing up her throat to push herself harder. She'd only taken three steps. "Sul—"

A bullet exploded from the chamber of Marrok's gun as Sullivan reached under his heavy coat. Then two more gunshots echoed throughout the clearing, each stealing more of her hope.

Sullivan dropped his backup weapon into the snow, reaching out for his brother, but it was too late. Marrok Warren collapsed to the ground, his own weapon falling from his grip. The breath she'd been holding rushed from her lungs. She'd seen too many of those kinds of injuries on tour. There was no saving his brother now.

Only the tree beside her kept Jane on her feet. Tears welled in her eyes. Her stomach rolled. Not for Marrok but because of the way Sullivan hovered over his brother's body. Nobody deserved to watch someone they loved die right in front of them. Hadn't Sullivan been betrayed enough? Jane pushed off from the tree, her arms tingling to wrap around him as he grieved.

A series of beeps rang from the vest.

Jane stopped cold. The message stretched across her chest had changed from *Armed* to a series of numbers. And they were counting down. She shot her head up, her survival instincts paralyzed. No. No, no, no, no. This wasn't happening. She wasn't an active bomb. An invisible elephant sat on her chest, and she couldn't think. Couldn't breathe.

"Jane!" Sullivan's features cleared through the fresh tears streaming down her face.

She stumbled back. No. She didn't want to die, but she wasn't going to be responsible for taking his life. Not Sullivan. Jane surveyed the trees. She wasn't an expert with explosives, but she was smart enough to know the closer he got, the more danger he was in. If she could get some distance, he might have a better chance of surviving the blast. Throwing her hands out, she backed toward the tree line. "Stay back! It's armed!"

He didn't listen, running straight at her. Those sea-blue eyes never left her as he closed in fast. "Elliot, get your tools!"

The private investigator ran for one of the Blackhawk Security SUVs.

She stumbled back into the tree she'd used for support mere moments ago and fell. They were going to try to disarm the bomb. They were going to put their lives on the line. For her. Jane checked the display. Less than two minutes. She lifted her gaze back to Sullivan. Blackmailing him, revealing his true identity to the police in an attempt to save his life, it'd all been a mistake. He had to know that. She'd never meant for any of this to happen. "I'm sorry. I'm so sorry."

She didn't know what else to say.

Sullivan dropped to his knees beside her. Darkness consumed his features, and her insides flipped. He moved in close, his hands sliding along the underside of her jaw. He threaded his fingers through the hair at the base of her skull, and goose bumps rose along her skin at his touch. With him this close, the surrounding air filling with his reassuring scent, she wanted nothing more than to sink into his hold. But they were running out of time. Literally. "Are you okay?"

Chaos and concern tinted Sullivan's words. Not a good combination.

"I'm fine." And it was the truth. At least in her last two minutes on earth, Jane had what she wanted. Sullivan Bishop. She framed his jawline with one hand. "But you need to get away from me. This thing—"

"Isn't going to blow with you in it." A growl vibrated through Sullivan's chest. "I promise."

"Okay." Any promise Sullivan made, he kept, but the tightness in her tendons connecting her neck and shoulders refused to believe him. Lacing her fingers between his, Jane nodded. They didn't have much time left before he had to start running. And she wasn't about to make any more mistakes with the man she'd fallen in love with. "I'm sorry. For everything. Breaking into your office, blackmailing you, going after Menas on my own. All of it. I'm sorry I dragged you into this. I'm sorry about Marrok."

Elliot slid onto his knees on her other side, out of breath but smiling. "Hello, gorgeous. Not dead again, I see. Always a plus." He pushed at her shoulder, putting her flat on her back. "Hand me the wire cutters," he said to Sullivan. "I'm going to need you to hold very still. You are literally a ticking time bomb, and any movement could set it off early."

"I'm not sorry." Sullivan thrust the cutters into his private investigator's hands. A slow smile spread across Sullivan's features as he squeezed her hand. "I thought the Full Metal Bitch had broken into my office, but, in reality, it was my future. You're my future, Jane, and I'm not going anywhere."

"I can't think when you're expressing your feelings, boss. It's unnatural." Elliot's voice held a word of caution as he sifted through countless wires and traced them to different points on the vest. "That was beautiful, by the way."

Did that mean Sullivan loved her, too? The remnants of cold drained from her body at his words. But Jane still unwound her fingers from his hand and shoved him back. "You need to run."

"The last time I left your side, my brother strapped you to this damn thing." He wrapped his hand in hers again and kissed the sensitive skin along the back. "I learn from my mistakes. And the police already know who I really am, so you have no other leverage to get rid of me. Ever again."

"There are too many wires." Elliot sat back on his heels. "We've got less than thirty seconds. Boss—"

"Then we're going to cut her out of it." Sullivan reached for the serrated blade tucked inside his boot. The world blurred as they flipped her onto her front. "I'm not giving up."

Blistering cold spread down into her bones as sounds of ripping fabric reached her ears. Adrenaline dumped into her veins and rocketed her heart rate higher as she prepared for the explosion. But she couldn't move on to the afterlife without telling the man she'd blackmailed how she felt. Jane reached for him. "Sullivan, no matter what happens, I need you to know… I love you."

He hesitated for a split second, his gaze softening. Sullivan tugged on the vest, cutting down the back. "I've got it!"

Sullivan hauled her upright. The weight of the vest pulled her to the ground, but she extracted her arms from the sleeve holes. The clock was still counting down. His grip tightened around her arm. He tossed the active vest far into the woods and tugged her after him. "Take cover!"

The rest of the Blackhawk Security team scattered behind the SUVs or the long line of snowbanks. Sullivan dragged her across the road and then pushed her ahead of him. "Get behind the tree line!"

A faint hum echoed through the trees.

Then the explosion erupted. The flames shot out behind them, the blast tossing them into the air. Terror ricocheted through her as Jane hit the ground and rolled. Twice. Three times. Smoke worked deep into her system when she came to a stop. She'd lost sight of Sullivan as darkness closed in around the edges of her vision. She stared up into the trees as mountains of snow fell from the branches above, burying her deeper while blackness closed in.

"Jane..."

## Chapter Fifteen

Probation and over two hundred hours of community service. Sullivan might've lost half of Blackhawk Security's clients thanks to Jane having him arrested for murder, but he also had the rest of his life to hold it over her head.

And he intended to do just that.

The hospital's white walls blurred together at the edges of his vision as he stalked toward Jane's room, the only room with an ex-Ranger stationed outside the door. It'd been a precaution in case his psychopathic brother had hired any other hit men who hadn't heard the news: Jane Reise was off-limits. And *his*.

"Hey, man." Nodding at Anthony in acknowledgment, Sullivan wrapped his hand around the doorknob. And froze. His nervous system flipped, a ball of tension gripping his stomach. The stitches in his arm and thigh where Marrok had shot him stretched, but it wasn't the pain keeping him in place. The birth certificate, Social Security card, driver's license and passport with Jane's picture she'd left in the Blackhawk Security SUV all said she'd planned on starting a new life. In California. What if, even after they'd neutralized the threat, even after he'd beaten murder charges, she hadn't changed her mind about leaving?

"I don't think I've seen your skin that shade of white before." Anthony might take refuge behind those sunglasses, but his apparent amusement stretched across his expression. "Boss."

"Do you blame me? Every time I'm around her, someone is either shooting at me or trying to blow me up." Not the truth, but Anthony didn't need to know differently. The possibility of Jane saying no to staying in Anchorage, of her taking back those three words she'd blurted when her life was in danger, constricted his hold on the doorknob. A slight sting in his side from where Christopher Menas had tried to gut him like a fish claimed his attention. He forced a smile. "I never thanked you for watching out for her. I appreciate it."

"You've always said you'd do anything to protect the team, and every one of us feels the same." Anthony shifted his weight and, for the first time, Sullivan noted a beaten gold ring hanging from around Anthony's neck, tucked behind the Kevlar vest. Glennon's ring. Anthony Harris, ex-Ranger and Blackhawk Security weapons expert, had been holding on to the love of his life all this time? He'd never said a word. Sullivan's heart sank. Surveying the hospital corridor, Anthony shoved the gold band under his shirt without making eye contact. "We don't agree with you keeping the fact she blackmailed you into all this from us, but if you love her, Jane Reise is part of this team. And we'll fight for her."

"Thanks again." The knot of tension in his gut dissipated. Not completely, but there was only one way to fix that. Because Sullivan wouldn't hang on to Jane like Anthony held on to the woman who'd walked out on him, never finding closure, always wondering if she was safe, but not being part of her life. He twisted the hospital room door handle, shouldering his way inside.

And all the air rushed from his lungs.

Jane pushed her arms through her jacket beside the hospital bed. He closed the door softly and watched her. The burns and cuts along her creamy skin had started healing, the dark circles he'd noted when they first met lighter than before. Her addictive vanilla scent filled the room, and Sullivan couldn't help but take a deep breath, holding on to her as long as he could. His Jane.

"You can stop staring at me any second now." Leveling that hazel gaze on him from over her shoulder, she smiled. Jane fixed her collar and turned toward him. "Unless you're here to tell me you're busting me out of this place a second time."

"I'm sure something could be arranged." In truth, her doctors had already cleared her to leave, but Sullivan shoved his hands into his jacket pockets and leveraged his weight back against the door. A few more minutes with her. That was all he needed. "Surviving a mercenary and my brother certainly looks good on you."

The brightness in her eyes dimmed for a split second, and that loss resurrected the gutting pain he'd felt when Menas had planted a knife in his rib cage.

"I'm so sorry about Marrok, Sullivan. You have no idea how much I wish he hadn't been involved. I never meant for any of this to happen." She rolled her lips between her teeth, her expression simply lost. She fidgeted with an invisible speck of dirt on her jacket. "You told me you didn't hate me before." She wrapped her arms across her midsection, almost as though she were preparing herself for the worst. "Have you changed your mind?"

"You deserve the truth." Sullivan closed the space between them slowly, giving her a chance to back away if she wanted. He could almost read her mind as the muscles along her spine sagged. Guilt. Shame. Regret. "Everything since that night has changed. For the first time in nineteen years, the world knows who I really am. And what I did. Because of you."

The color drained from her face. Her jaw slackened. Jane swiped at her face, her attention on the door over his shoulder, then moved to maneuver around him. "I understand."

"No, you don't." Sullivan clamped a hand around her arm and spun her into his chest. For the first time, she didn't fight, and he took that as a good sign. Staring down at her, he locked her in his hold. She wasn't going anywhere. At least, not without him. "If you understood, you wouldn't keep running away from me. None of this was your fault, Jane. You can't control other people's behavior. You did your job like you were supposed to."

Spreading his fingers along her jaw, he fought back the memories of Marrok in his final moments. And the thought of almost losing Jane to the bomb his brother had strapped to her chest. It shouldn't have gone down like that, but there'd been no way to see the real threat before discovering his brother's pen in that photo. "As much as I hate to admit what he was capable of, Marrok made his own decisions, and he paid for them."

"And what about the fact I turned you in to the police for murder?" Her voice was so soft, soft and vulnerable, and Sullivan's insides contracted. She refused to look at him, setting her palms against his beating heart. "Is the Full Metal Bitch going to be credited with bringing down Blackhawk Security's CEO? Because…" She picked at his shirt. "I'm not that person anymore, Sullivan, and I don't want you, of all people, to believe I am."

"I'm not in love with a heartless woman who would do anything in her power to bring down hardworking soldiers. I'm in love with *you*, the real Jane Reise." He moved a strand of hair off her cheek, hugging her closer. "You're determined, yes. Willing to do whatever it takes to get what you want, but I think that's what I love about you the most. You're caring and brave. And I can't imagine a better woman by my side."

A smile stretched across her features. "Don't forget saving your life two more times."

"How could I? Lucky for you, the district attorney and I came to an agreement. No prison time, considering the circumstances of who my father was and Marrok's second death." Sullivan breathed a little easier at the thought but still tightened his hold on the woman in his arms. He might never have laid eyes on her again had the DA not taken recent events into account. "He hit me with community service and probation as long I promise not to exact vigilante justice again."

"A little late for that, isn't it?" A small puff of laughter burst from her lips, as she finally looked up at him. Fisting the collar of his jacket in her hands, she shoved against him and pulled him back in. "Is that a promise you think you can keep?"

"I keep all my promises. You know that." He traced his fingertips across her jaw. Jane's breathing pattern changed. Because of him. Because of his touch. And his body hummed with the possibility of experimenting with her reactions for the rest of their lives. "But if I have to break that promise to keep you safe, Jane, I will. Whether there's a possibility of me going to prison or not."

"All right. Then I'll make a promise, too." The darkness in her beauty vanished, replaced with warmth, hope and so much more. The burden she'd hung on to for the last few months had been lifted, and Sullivan loved the effect. "Whatever happens after we walk out those hospital doors, I promise never to blackmail you into helping me again."

Whatever happened? She'd meant it as a joke, but confusion closed in on him, and Sullivan backed off a step. "If by 'whatever happens,' you mean you walking out those doors with me and signing the paperwork for your permanent transfer to Anchorage."

"Sullivan…" Jane let her hands fall to her sides, and everything inside him went cold. "Haven't you learned your lesson yet? Forget prison. Loving me is a *death* sentence. And I'm not going to be the one responsible for taking your life. I think I've screwed it up enough."

She couldn't be serious. Not after everything they'd been through. Sliding his hands through his hair, Sullivan turned away to hide the obvious fire burning through his veins. Because he couldn't stand the thought of her walking away from this. From him. "So saying you loved me when Elliot was trying to disarm that bomb strapped to your chest was some attempt to… What?" He took a deep breath, trying to clear her scent from his system, but she was all around him. She was in his veins. "Put my mind at ease in case you died?"

"No—" she swiped her tongue across her bottom lip, and his heart rate kicked up a notch "—of course not. I—"

"What you do with your life is up to you, Jane. I would never force you into anything you're not comfortable with. If you don't want to stay here in Anchorage, fine. That's your choice." He stalked toward her, craving the feel of her against him, but he caged the desire racking his nervous system. He pushed every ounce of raw passion he held for the woman who'd blackmailed him into his voice. "But just because you're holding on to your guilt with everything you have does not give you the right to make the decision of what I do with my life or who gets to stay in it."

Sullivan rolled his fingers into fists when all he wanted to do was grab her by the arms and commit every inch of her body to memory all over again. His heart worked to beat out of his chest. He took a deep breath. Two. The fire simmered to a slow burn. There, but manageable. He relaxed his hands, trailing the pad of his thumb across her full bottom lip, the one she always licked when she was nervous. "When I said everything has changed since that night under the aurora borealis, it's not that I changed my mind. It's that I'm scared as hell to love you, Jane, but here I am, in love with you anyway."

Sliding one hand into his jacket pocket, he extracted the documents she'd had made under a different name and tossed them onto the bed without taking his eyes off her. "Now all you have to do is stay."

Stay?

Her lips parted as she caught sight of the documents, and her mouth went dry. The pulse at the base of her neck quickened. She closed her eyes for a split second. She'd left them in the Blackhawk Security SUV she'd stolen from Anthony at the hospital. Sullivan's weapons expert must've recovered them and handed them over to his boss after Marrok had taken her.

The hair on the back of her neck stood at attention as the memories flashed across her mind. The bomb's beeping as Marrok had set the countdown into motion played over and over in her head. Pressing her fingers into her eye sockets, she attempted to relieve the pressure building behind her eyes. But the look of horror on Sullivan's face as he realized what his brother had done had ingrained itself into her mind. Forever. "I need…"

What did she need?

"Jane," he said.

His voice slid through her, drowning out the nightmare that'd brought them together, and she couldn't help but step into his arms. His body heat worked down through her clothing, deep into her bones, as she set her ear against his heart. She interlaced her fingers at the small of his back, terrified to let go. "I need...you." Her own words echoed throughout her mind as she recalled her reasons for seeking Sullivan out in the first place. "I need you."

"You have me. But I can't live the rest of my life wondering what would've happened if I let you walk away now. I love you. I want you to stay." He set his cheek against the crown of her head, his clean, masculine scent surrounding her, working down into her pores. "So what is it going to be, Jane?"

The tension hardening the muscles along her spine dissipated as he wrapped his thick arms around her, and she sank further into him. Was this how it would always be between them? This give and take, this passion to keep each other from getting hurt?

From the second she'd broken into Sullivan Bishop's office, she swore not to let her heart rule her decision making, but the rules of blackmail had gone out the window one by one over the past days. He'd saved her life, protected her from a group of mercenaries for crying out loud and put his future at risk. All for her. And in her last perceived moments on this earth, she'd trusted her gut to tell him exactly what her head refused to acknowledge. She loved him.

She wasn't sure when it'd happened, maybe only now, but she'd decided she wanted him more than she was afraid of losing him.

His heart pounded hard against her ear, strong and reliant. He was a SEAL. And he could take care of himself. No matter the threat, Sullivan Bishop protected those he cared about and always seemed to stay alive in the process. Jane tightened her hold on him. And that would have to be enough. "I love you, too."

He pushed her back a few inches, trying to fight the smile curling at the edge of his mouth. Sullivan gripped her around the waist. His eyes brightened as the smile overwhelmed his expression, and Jane's heart stuttered. "Really?"

"Yes. And I'm staying. With you." She nodded. Her gut instincts said this was the right choice. This was where she wanted to be. "Unless you need someone to drag you to safety through the middle of the Alaskan wilderness again, then you're on your own."

Sullivan framed her jawline between his strong hands and crushed his mouth to hers. She tried to breathe around the rush of desire flooding through her. He'd worked his way under her skin, branded himself on her soul, and her body's response to him slipped further and further out of her control. He caressed her lower back and lifted her off her feet, pressing her against him as though he intended to make them one. And she might've had a few ideas herself on how to make that happen. Injuries be damned. This was where she wanted to be.

He swept his tongue inside her mouth, laying claim. He kissed her with a wild, desperate passion and Jane took everything he gave. Arms wrapped around his neck, she clung to him as months of fear and paranoia drained from her muscles.

She had her life back. Because the one man she'd needed the most had kept his promise. Because of Sullivan.

"Is it necessary to hold that woman so tight?" a familiar voice asked.

They turned toward Elliot in the door frame, cheeks pressed together, but Sullivan kept her in his arms. A growl vibrated from deep in Sullivan's chest as he eased her back to her feet. "This better be important."

Pressed against him, Jane enjoyed the funny things that growl did to her insides but wiped at her mouth and pulled her T-shirt down over her jeans' waistband. Heat worked up her neck and into her face the longer the private investigator smiled at them.

"The police want your statements about what went down at the cabin." Elliot hiked a thumb over his shoulder. "Should I tell them to give you another thirty minutes?"

Another growl echoed throughout the room.

"Okay, okay. Forty-five minutes." Blackhawk Security's private investigator spun on his heel and wrenched open the door. How she hadn't heard him come in in the first place, Jane would never know.

"You know, Jane, I was actually worried you would be too late in telling him how you felt, and we were all going to die." Elliot turned back before hitting the hallway, and that crooked smile of his warned Jane she wasn't about to like what came out of his mouth next. "I'm glad everything worked out for the best."

"Come again?" Narrowing his eyes, Sullivan stepped toward the private investigator with fire burning hot in his gaze, but Jane held him back.

"Wait a second. Do you mean to tell me you knew which wire to cut prior to Sullivan cut-

ting me out of the vest? And the only reason
you waited was because I hadn't told him how I
felt yet?" Heat surged through her. Forget about
Sullivan beating Elliot to a pulp. She'd kill him
herself. Jane crossed the room. Grabbing the
private investigator by the collar, she hauled
him close. "Are you insane? We almost died!"

"I knew you'd do the right thing when it
came down to the wire. No pun intended."
That crooked, cocky smile deepened the laugh
lines around Elliot's mouth, but, as his attention
shifted over Jane's shoulder—to Sullivan—the
smile disappeared.

She didn't have to turn around to know her
SEAL was considering ways to use his tightly
honed skills in torture on his private investigator. Tension filled the hospital room, and she
didn't see any way out for Elliot other than re-
signing from his job and going into hiding for
the rest of his life. Jane unclenched her hold on
his collar and moved out of the way. "You better start running now."

Elliot's coffee-colored eyes widened as Sullivan closed in.

"Now, boss, we're friends, right? I owe you
my life. I was using the bomb as an incentive."
Elliot backed toward the door, hands held up
in defense, but Jane didn't hold her SEAL back

this time. "Keep in mind I gave you plenty of time to cut her out of the vest in case she didn't want to express how she felt."

"The next time I see you better be on a plane to Iraq, Dunham." Sullivan stalked after him, danger and rage rising in each step.

Elliot ran out the door as fast as he could. No looking back. Probably a good decision on his part. His voice slid through the crack in the door as he bolted down the hallway. "You should be thanking me!"

The tightness remained across Sullivan's back, but Jane couldn't help but thread her arms around his waist.

"Give him a head start before you kill him." A laugh bubbled from her lips as Jane sank into the comfort of Sullivan's strong, muscled back. He spun in her grasp, pinning her with those sea-blue eyes she couldn't get enough of.

"There's still one thing we need to get clear on before we walk out those doors together." His expression sobered as he stared down at her, and Jane tightened her grip on him. "And after what happened with Menas and my brother, I think I have the right to know."

"Are you sure you're up for another interroga-tion? I seem to recall me winning the last one." Caution narrowed her gaze. She didn't have any more secrets. At least, none that would get them killed. But she trusted him with her life. If he wanted to interrogate her before jumping into the most dangerous assignment of his career— a relationship with her—all he had to do was ask. Echoes from the PA system filtered into the room, but Jane had attention for only the wide expanse of muscle under her fingertips. "I'll tell you anything."

"That's a good start. Because I have ways of making you talk." His voice was deep and dark, and it sent an instinct of warning down her spine. But then Sullivan raised his hand a split second before he dropped a piece of ice down her T-shirt.

Freezing water dripped down her spine. Jane screamed, trying to dislodge the ice cube, but it'd caught in her sports bra. "Where the heck did you get ice?"

"I paid Elliot five dollars to come in and tell you that whole thing about the bomb as a distraction so I could lift a piece of ice from your side table." A gut-wrenching smile spread across Sullivan's features as he wrapped her in his arms.

"So what he said wasn't true?" she asked.

"No." Sullivan shook his head. "I'm pretty

sure I would've already broken my promise to the district attorney had any of that been true."

The ice fell from her shirt, and she slapped at his shoulder. "Oh, this isn't over. When we get back to the cabin, you're going to need me to save you from the brink of death in front of the fire again."

"Mmm. I like that idea." He purred into her ear, the tip of his nose tracing the most sensitive part of her neck. "But, really, tell me how you broke into Blackhawk Security. I've had my network security team run diagnostics on my entire security system—three times—and they haven't come back with a single loophole. Either you paid someone to let you in, which your financials can't prove, or you're more than what you seem, Counselor."

"All right, Frogman, you want to know?" He'd fought like hell for her, nearly died for her—more times than she could count—and lost a brother all over again in the process. At this point, she'd give him anything he asked for. And not just the truth. Everything she had. Everything she was. And she would fight like hell for him for the rest of their lives.

"More than anything," he said.

"It's really eating you up inside, isn't it? Okay then." She crooked her finger at him, putting her mouth right next to Sullivan's ear as he leaned in. His scent washed over her, and she took a deep breath. He wanted answers, but Jane wanted more. She wanted forever. With him. A smile spread her lips thin, and she dropped the ice cube down the back of his shirt. "Did you think it was going to be that easy?"

Sullivan jerked away, his laugh loud enough to echo down the hall. Locking that enthralling blue gaze on her, he stalked toward her, all SEAL, all predator. All hers. "Oh, this is going to be fun."

\* \* \* \* \*

# Get 4 FREE REWARDS!

## We'll send you 2 FREE Books plus 2 FREE Mystery Gifts.

**Harlequin® Romantic Suspense** books feature heart-racing sensuality and the promise of a sweeping romance set against the backdrop of suspense.

FREE
Value Over
**$20**

---

**YES!** Please send me 2 FREE Harlequin® Romantic Suspense novels and my 2 FREE gifts (gifts are worth about $10 retail). After receiving them, if I don't wish to receive any more books, I can return the shipping statement marked "cancel." If I don't cancel, I will receive 4 brand-new novels every month and be billed just $4.99 per book in the U.S. or $5.74 per book in Canada. That's a savings of at least 12% off the cover price! It's quite a bargain! Shipping and handling is just 50¢ per book in the U.S. and 75¢ per book in Canada*. I understand that accepting the 2 free books and gifts places me under no obligation to buy anything. I can always return a shipment and cancel at any time. The free books and gifts are mine to keep no matter what I decide.

240/340 HDN GMYZ

Name (please print)

Address                                                                                  Apt. #

City                                  State/Province                          Zip/Postal Code

### Mail to the **Reader Service**:
**IN U.S.A.:** P.O. Box 1341, Buffalo, NY 14240-8531
**IN CANADA:** P.O. Box 603, Fort Erie, Ontario L2A 5X3

**Want to try two free books from another series! Call 1-800-873-8635 or visit www.ReaderService.com.**

HRS18

# Get 4 FREE REWARDS!

## We'll send you 2 FREE Books
## plus 2 FREE Mystery Gifts.

**Presents**

USA TODAY BESTSELLING AUTHOR
**Dani Collins**

Consequence of His Revenge

**Presents**

USA TODAY BESTSELLING AUTHOR
**Melanie Milburne**

Blackmailed into the Marriage Bed

**Harlequin Presents®** books feature a sensational and sophisticated world of international romance where sinfully tempting heroes ignite passion.

**FREE**
Value Over
**$20**

**YES!** Please send me 2 FREE Harlequin Presents® novels and my 2 FREE gifts (gifts are worth about $10 retail). After receiving them, if I don't wish to receive any more books, I can return the shipping statement marked "cancel." If I don't cancel, I will receive 6 brand-new novels every month and be billed just $4.55 each for the regular-print edition or $5.55 each for the larger-print edition in the U.S., or $5.49 each for the regular-print edition or $5.99 each for the larger-print edition in Canada. That's a savings of at least 11% off the cover price! It's quite a bargain! Shipping and handling is just 50¢ per book in the U.S. and 75¢ per book in Canada*. I understand that accepting the 2 free books and gifts places me under no obligation to buy anything. I can always return a shipment and cancel at any time. The free books and gifts are mine to keep no matter what I decide.

Choose one: ☐ **Harlequin Presents®**
Regular-Print
(106/306 HDN GMYX)

☐ **Harlequin Presents®**
Larger-Print
(176/376 HDN GMYX)

Name (please print)

Address                                                                    Apt. #

City                                  State/Province                      Zip/Postal Code

Mail to the **Reader Service:**
IN U.S.A.: P.O. Box 1341, Buffalo, NY 14240-8531
IN CANADA: P.O. Box 603, Fort Erie, Ontario L2A 5X3

Want to try two free books from another series! Call **1-800-873-8635** or visit www.ReaderService.com.

*Terms and prices subject to change without notice. Prices do not include applicable taxes. Sales tax applicable in N.Y. Canadian residents will be charged applicable taxes. Offer not valid in Quebec. This offer is limited to one order per household. Books received may not be as shown. Not valid for current subscribers to Harlequin Presents books. All orders subject to approval. Credit or debit balances in a customer's account(s) may be offset by any other outstanding balance owed by or to the customer. Please allow 4 to 6 weeks for delivery. Offer available while quantities last.

**Your Privacy**—The Reader Service is committed to protecting your privacy. Our Privacy Policy is available online at www.ReaderService.com or upon request from the Reader Service. We make a portion of our mailing list available to reputable third parties that offer products we believe may interest you. If you prefer that we not exchange your name with third parties, or if you wish to clarify or modify your communication preferences, please visit us at www.ReaderService.com/consumerchoice or write to us at Reader Service Preference Service, P.O. Box 9062, Buffalo, NY 14240-9062. Include your complete name and address.

HP18

# READERSERVICE.COM

## Manage your account online!

- Review your order history
- Manage your payments
- Update your address

> **We've designed the
> Reader Service website
> just for you.**

## Enjoy all the features!

- Discover new series available to you, and read excerpts from any series.
- Respond to mailings and special monthly offers.
- Browse the Bonus Bucks catalog and online-only exculsives.
- Share your feedback.

**Visit us at:**
# ReaderService.com